Soldier in the Grass

Joanna Crispi

[signature: joanna crispi]

Books™

The New York Quarterly Foundation, Inc.
New York, New York

NYQ Books™ is an imprint of The New York Quarterly Foundation, Inc.

The New York Quarterly Foundation, Inc.
P. O. Box 2015
Old Chelsea Station
New York, NY 10113

www.nyqbooks.org

First Edition

Set in Myriad Pro

Layout and Design by Raymond P. Hammond
Cover Photo: Hannes Steyn/Flickr/Getty Images

Library of Congress Control Number: 2009927388

ISBN: 978-1-935520-00-9

Soldier in the Grass

CHAPTER ONE

"Just a little while." He heard the voice inside his head as he lay on the cool grass beneath a sky dripping with stars. He felt hot and cold in the same instant, felt his teeth knocking against one another and the sweat on his back. And he heard a voice that spoke to him out of the night, "You thought I had forsaken you."

When he awoke, it was light. The African sun was burning his eyes. There was a woman kneeling over him. He felt her fingers pressing against his wrist.

"You're not well," she said.

Her hand rested on his feverish brow.

"Can you stand?" she asked.

He tried to lift himself, but everything turned dark despite the bright sun.

She reached out and helped him to his feet. He tried not to lean on her, but he felt his legs giving way, and he clutched his arm across her back as they walked.

There was a house not far from where they were. Last night, in the dark he could not see it.

She led him to a bedroom separated from the kitchen by a folding door.

"Lie down," she said. "Let me help you with your boots."

He felt a chill run through his body again, and he groped for the blanket.

"You have a fever," she said. She placed the quinine pills in his mouth one at a time, the pills dissolving in small sips of water as she held the glass to his lips.

Where was he? And who was she, the woman with the face like an angel, why was she helping him?

But he could not hold on to any thought; the fire inside him seemed to burn them up. Then there was nothing, sleep perhaps, until the next burst of images.

"*Il fait froid,*" he muttered, though it was his mother's voice he heard in the room instead of his own. His mother complained of the cold. How many nights later did she die? Not nights, but months, her shivering body clinging to his for warmth in that bed where the sheets were worn from being washed too often in a futile attempt to wash the odor of sickness from the room. He was a child then.

He felt himself slipping back into sleep, the sound of his mother's voice receded into silence.

When he opened his eyes, the woman was still there. "*O`u suis-je?*" he asked.

His lips were cracked from sun and fever, and his arms were covered with welts from mosquitoes.

"Two hundred kilometers northwest of Brazzaville," she said quietly.

He closed his eyes.

She washed the caked mud and dirt from his face and arms. The odor of fire and dried blood was in his hair and on his clothes. From time to time he opened his eyes and looked at her, his eyes glistening with fever as if he were trying to remember or understand something. Though she tried to talk to him, he was delirious.

Over the next hour his condition seemed to worsen. His body burned to the touch. The skin around his eyes appeared so dark, it looked bruised. His ashen lips curled back over his teeth.

She cooled his back and legs with a washcloth, soaking the cloth over and over as the fever burned it dry until she herself was weak from the heat. Little moans escaped from his lips as if he were having a nightmare. Then he began to shiver again. All of her efforts seemed in vain.

Out of fatigue, she stopped to rest. She felt the heat from his body travel through her fingers up her arm. "What would happen if he died?" The thought frightened her and she forced it from her mind.

She went outside to the pump and splashed water over her face and hair to cool off. Shielding her eyes from the sun with her hand, she surveyed the empty grounds and the plateau beyond it, desolate as always. In the silence, she had found it hard to take the warnings of war seriously. But now as the French soldier lay dying in her bed, the war had come to her.

When she returned, he was tossing and moaning loudly.

"De l'eau, de l'eau—"

He wanted water. He was too weak to sit up on his own. She lifted his head and held the glass to his lips. He drank until it was empty and fell back listlessly on the pillow.

Somewhere in the near distance there was an explosion followed by gunfire.

By late afternoon he went into a drenching sweat. The sheets were soaked, and she lifted him onto his side as she replaced the sheet with a dry one. He seemed limp, as if he were a mass of flesh held together only by her arms. Gently, she placed his body back down on the dry sheet. He touched her weakly on the wrist and opened his eyes as she covered him. A moment later he seemed to have drifted into sleep.

She pulled the mosquito netting over the bed. Before then she had not noticed his face. He was handsome, she thought. His forehead protruded slightly over his long, gray eyes. He had a straight nose that widened a little at the bottom, giving it a sensual appearance, a strong, defined jaw, and a beautifully shaped mouth; the upper lip was curved and full. Something about him touched her.

She left him and went out onto the veranda. Though it was evening, she had no appetite, only the desire for tea, which she drank hot as she watched the sun going down in a hazy sky.

There was another volley of gunfire, but it was somewhere in the distance.

CHAPTER TWO

It was nearly dawn when he awoke. He heard the annoying whine of a mosquito close to his face and he lay very still, listening to the sound becoming louder until it was deafening as a siren. He tried to kill it, but lifting his arm involved a gesture beyond his strength.

The fever had left him confused and exhausted. He had forgotten about the woman, until in the half-light he saw her asleep in a chair across from him. In his mind he tried to piece together the events of the last seventy-two hours, though he had no idea how much time had passed. Then events began to come back to him. Not in any order, but they were the right events at least.

He remembered the convent where they had evacuated the nuns that morning. They were old, most of them, and terribly frightened, clutching their prayer beads in their hands as they were led away. Sister Bernadette held his arm. There were explosions in the distance and a shudder of fear stopped her in her tracks.

When he tried to console her, she answered, "I'm not afraid for myself, it's the thought of what horror has just befallen some poor person that makes me shudder."

As if in answer to the silent thought of life's awfulness that passed across his eyes, she said, "He is my God, and I believe in Him."

The nuns had been collecting the fallen bullets and pieces of shrapnel after each attack. They kept them in an aluminum pail and handed them to the soldiers as if it were some valuable piece of evidence.

"You slept for a long time."

The mosquito netting obscured her face. Then he remembered her leaning over him with the wet cloth.

"*Je ne te connais pas.*"

"*Je suis Angeline Bousquet.*"

Her name is Angeline. "When we lose the glow of life, we see the light of angels" —he had heard that somewhere, though he no longer knew where. Now, looking at her, he thought of it again.

He caught sight of his bare chest and thighs, and looked up with embarrassment before covering himself with the sheet.

"Your clothes were covered with blood," she said.

He forced himself to sit up; he felt dizzy and his back ached.

"I am Vincent Chavanne. I am a Lieutenant in the Foreign Legion," he said out of a need to reassure her, though she seemed at ease with his being there. "I am on a mission for the government of France."

His gaze darted across the room. "How long have I been here?" he asked.

"I found you yesterday."

"What day is this?"

"Monday."

"My regiment arrived in Brazzaville on the ninth of June. My section broke out into the countryside for reconnaissance. We were caught in a rebel ambush."

He looked down at the blistered insides of his hands as he recreated the scene in his mind.

They were pretty far from Brazzaville. A band of black men in fatigues and tee shirts with sunglasses and scarves tied around their heads stood across the dirt road pointing *Kalashnikovs*, the heavy Russian rifles left over from the years of Communism. When they opened fire, he took cover behind the jeep and fired off a round from a *"douze-sept"*. He remembered promising himself he was not going to die—not then, not in this hell-hole of a country.

"Lt. Chavanne?" someone called out to him and he turned. That's when he saw the girl, a child, barefoot, in a flimsy, yellow cotton shift. She came running, raised her arms and hurled something. Then the explosion went off.

Angeline interrupted his thoughts. "Something must have frightened them," she said. "They left your boots, which are considered a prize. They must have seen the spirit of the dead man on top of you."

In the Legion no one referred to them as boots; it was always "Rangers." They were unique to the French Combat regiments, and a pair of boots like those would have been a prize.

"What happened to the soldiers with you?" she asked.

"I'm not sure. At least one of us was already dead when the grenade went off." He stopped for a moment, lowered his eyes, even if he had known the girl was carrying a grenade, he doubted whether he could have fired at her; she was only a child.

"I headed away from the road into the wilderness. Somehow I arrived here."

It sounded so easy as he said it, as if the madness and despair of exhaustion and fever were already gone from his memory. He remembered coming to in the pitch dark, feeling a weight on top of him as if someone had dropped a slab of rock; he thought he had been crushed beneath the *velera*. A few minutes passed before he realized it was a body. He got out, and crawled on the ground. It was pitch dark and he stumbled over a piece of the engine. Then he started to run.

It was becoming light; he could make out her face more clearly. She had a pretty, Mediterranean face, with a full, sensuous mouth, high cheekbones, a nice nose and the palest green eyes he had ever seen, not at all deep set but open, diaphanous, observant, yet warm, against dark lashes and long gently arching eyebrows. "Talking eyes," was the way to describe eyes like hers, he thought; her face could remain perfectly still and yet she could say everything with her eyes.

"You must be hungry," she said.

He was weak from hunger. "Yes. Very," he answered, adding, "I don't want to deprive you. I'm already indebted to you."

" You've given me something to do. I was lonely here by myself."

She handed him a cotton robe from atop the dresser.

"Wear this for now. I'll get you clean pants and a shirt."

When she stood he noticed she was smaller than he would have thought, something about her, her long full brown hair, her watchful eyes, the width of her shoulders, gave an impression of someone who was taller.

The smell of the omelet filled up the room, a delicious aroma of fried onions and olive oil. She put bread and honey on the table.

The first few sips of coffee raced through his blood to his head, and he felt a warm flush, as if his whole body were awakening from the stupor of the fever. He ate without looking up like someone who has been starved, wiping his plate with the hard bread and washing it down with coffee.

"How far out from Brazzaville are you?"

"Half day's drive by four wheel vehicle. Not far for Africa. Impfondo, the next major city along the Congo, is about two days away by ferry."

She got up and went to the stove for the coffee pot, refilling his bowl to the top.

"You have arrived at a coffee plantation. Offering you coffee is easy," she said. She spoke in a soft, dignified voice, yet her eyes lit up her words.

"You've been very kind. Another person would have left me out there."

"My husband left for Paris before this started. Nobody expected it. We believed Pascal Lissouba's reelection was certain. Is it true; the Zulu and Cobra militias have overtaken Brazzaville? The rebels are acting on behalf of Nguesso, who is Marxist. Lissouba overthrew him. Now the cycle starts all over again."

Before she spoke of her husband, he had not noticed the thin gold wedding band on her finger.

"It must be frightening for you to be alone here," he said.

Her pale green eyes met his. She had a direct way of looking at him.

"I was not alone," she said, flicking the ash from her cigarette and taking a last drag before putting it out and handing the ashtray to him. "What was it like in Brazzaville?" she asked.

"I saw a mob of six men in broad daylight lift a man and throw him off a bridge. A summary execution they said. I asked them what he had done. One man answered: 'He was not one of us,' and they moved on."

He paused, considering whether to say more; the incident weighed on his mind. "We were given orders not to take sides, not to engage. We had to watch as they killed one another. I could shoot a dog if it attacked a corpse, but I could not stop them from throwing that man over the bridge."

She said, "You would have acted if the man had been white."

"I am a soldier; I take orders. I also know that my actions have political significance. I act for France, not for my conscience."

"And you don't exist? Only France?"

"What I think is irrelevant."

She said, "You would not know how to choose sides. You have to live here before you know such things."

The accusatory tone left her voice. "The radio gave out a warning for all *colons* to remain at home; it's not safe to be white out of doors now. The ninety-three war was different. Whites were off limits."

"They're right, it isn't safe."

He said nothing more, though the image came to his mind of the streets lined with shattered glass glistening in the hot sun and the stench of corpses left for days. When they removed the dead they had no eyes because the birds had pecked them out.

"This property is well known among the villages. We have 50 hectares, unusually large for Congo where it is mostly small family farms. The commercial plantations disappeared during the years of communism. We employ thirty people during the harvest. They come by pick-up truck, as many as can stand in the back. Patrick gave the truck to the foreman, because otherwise they would have to walk two hours in the sun each way."

"Patrick is your husband?"

"Yes, he works with the oil companies out of Pointe-Noire. He is Belgian. Like me, he was born here. The plantation serves his purpose. He is not just another European poacher, here for the oil, so he is trusted."

They heard the first explosion of gunfire in the nearby distance. He noticed she did not blink. It was something he had been taught in training camp: if a soldier blinks, he dies.

"You were pretty far from the house when you found me," he said. "Where were you going?"

"I was checking on the trees, like any morning. I find it reassuring, as if everything had returned to normal. When I was a child I used to play in the shade of the trees all day. I feel safe there."

There was another explosion, followed by silence. She pushed the hair back from her face. Her brow was damp with perspiration.

"Where were you when your vehicle was blown up?"

"North of Loubomo, about a hundred-fifty kilometers northwest of Brazzaville. "

"We are to the north, roughly two hours by car, maybe more depending on conditions, in the hills between Brazzaville and Loubomo."

Her property was not that far out from Brazzaville. The thought passed through his mind; why hadn't she been evacuated?

"French troops have not been here?" he asked.

"No, but now they will come. They will come looking for you. 'Leave no man behind,'—I remember reading somewhere—it's the motto of the Legion, isn't it?"

"*Tu n'abandonnes jamais ni tes morts, ni tes blesses, ni tes armes,*" he said.

He smiled wide enough for his teeth to show, the prominent front teeth and the bottom teeth which overlapped slightly. When he smiled his eyes turned up at the corners and he had a dimple on his right cheek; the melancholy disappeared and there was an insouciance and an irresistible charm to his face. His eyes were the color of the brooding sky, full of light, impossible not to notice, overwhelming everything about his appearance, the gaunt face, spotty beard.

"They will come, you'll see," he said, confidently.

"You would probably like a shower," she said. "There is one outside. Come, I'll show you."

She got up, gesturing with her hand for him to follow her.

He stopped her. "My gun was stolen," he said. "I'd feel better if I had a gun."

She opened a drawer in the kitchen and took out a semi-automatic Beretta. "I've been carrying this," she said, handing it to him.

He looked at it for a moment before handing it back to her.

"Keep it," she said. "You'll feel safe. I have another. Here everything is in short supply except guns."

CHAPTER THREE

From her window she could see him at the shower. In that first glimpse, as the towel slipped down his hips onto the damp tile, she knew she should turn away, but she did not. Instead she remained by the window watching as he showered, his naked body, lean, muscular and unabashed, standing alone against the immense landscape and the sky streaked with rust at the borders of the horizon. Somewhere the bush was burning, tinting the sky, and she felt breathless in the stifling air.

The gunfire had stopped, not long enough for the birds to begin flying again. But long enough to notice that it was silent. She remembered those first days, waking to her empty house and looking down from the hill to the tops of the trees below, wondering what harm lay hidden and waiting beneath the trees.

She unlocked the drawer to the nightstand and took out a revolver. The soldier was right. Here everyone needs a gun, she thought. She examined the gun before turning it to a loaded chamber and putting it back in the drawer. Then she took out a long cedar box where she kept her mother and father's wedding rings tied together with a ribbon, a child's gold cross with a tiny diamond in the center ("So it gleams in the light like the spirit of God," her father had said) given to her for her seventh birthday and the only photo she had of her parents with her brother, Joachim. It was before she was born, father, mother, brother, they were smiling in the picture. Then Joachim died and she was born and everyone stopped smiling. These were not the things she was looking for, though she could not help feeling sad whenever she saw them. It was something else, twenty-thousand francs, hidden beneath a sliding tray at the bottom of the cedar box. She took the money out and folded it inside a small jewelry sack.

From what the soldier had said she concluded the French should be close by. An old brown leather suitcase lay open at the foot of the bed. It had been two days, but she had not been able to take the next step of packing.

She knelt over the empty suitcase. She wanted to cry, but she felt something hard inside of her that prevented her, as if she had no right to feel the way she did. She had lived in the Congo too long to believe in entitlement.

"Où est Maman?" She had felt entitled to an answer on the day her father arrived alone at the girls' school run by the nuns in Brazzaville. They sat together in the garden filled with forsythia and poinsettia. Her father had dark brown eyes that sloped down at the corners, which Africans believed to be a sign of ambition. If her father had been ambitious, it had passed long before that morning.

"Your mother has gone to France. She is not coming back."

How hard it must have been for him to say those words. He took her hand as if he expected her to cry, but she did not.

"She will make arrangements to send for you at the end of the term," he said. But she never did. She died before the term ended.

She thought of her mother's funeral. It was always that image she associated with leaving Africa. Standing in the cold rain, not hearing the prayers, only the splatter of the rain against the wet mud, *City of Light*, it rained every day they were there, and she remembered thinking, now it is all right to cry; no one will notice in all this rain. *How much longer until it is over, Papa? Soon. Soon. Maman will be happy to be buried under a Paris sky.* Then she remembered hiding her face beneath his coat as they walked, to shield against the cold and the damp and the triste gray sky closing around her.

A spider had begun crawling its way across the top of the suitcase, moving forward on its thin, nearly transparent legs, like the strings that pull a marionette. Not a poisonous spider—a harmless bite, the poisonous ones were always heavier with thicker legs—yet silent and malevolent, intruding on her like a voyeur. She knocked it to the floor and crushed it with her sandal.

She believed this rebellion was no different than the others. She had already survived a half dozen. It was like living near a river that flooded—something that had to be endured from time to time. Now that the French had sent soldiers, the rebels would desist. In a few days her workers would return to work. The airports would open and Patrick would return from Paris. It was always the same, a bribe in the right amount to the right person.

She felt a surge of doubt before her thoughts went blank. Her hand on her brow was damp from sweat. She glanced back through the window. The soldier had finished his shower and was walking back to the house.

CHAPTER FOUR

Vincent found a white linen shirt and khaki trousers on the bed when he came in from the shower. Judging from the clothes, he guessed her husband was about his size; the pants were big at the waist, but at the moment his own clothes would have fallen off too.

He took the Beretta with him. It was quiet in the house, and he assumed she was sleeping. He wanted to check for possible entrance and escape ways. The rooms were large, sparsely furnished, a few chairs and two small canopies facing one another, the walls a yellowed white, the paint cracked across the ceilings where the plaster had given way to too much heat and light.

There was a library in an alcove off the reception room. Shelves of books lined the walls. The front leg of the bamboo writing desk was pitched forward as if it had cracked. Two black-and-white photographs rested atop the desk in small silver frames, pictures of Angeline as a little girl, the only photographs he had come across in the house.

He picked them up one at a time. In the first he guessed she was about five years old, dressed in a sailor dress, and the photograph, which appeared to have been taken in a photographer's studio, seemed intended to commemorate some special event, though he could not tell from the photo what the occasion might have been. Her face has not changed since then, he thought, the large eyes staring boldly into the camera, she seemed confident and poised, her expression that of an adult rather than a child. In the second photograph she could have been no more than three years old. She held her father's hand and was smiling, a luminous smile that held back nothing.

He tried to rub some of the tarnish off the silver frame with his finger. Putting the photograph back on the desk, he thought back to his own childhood. He was eight when his mother died, from then he was sent to military school, and thus began the soldier's life from which he had never strayed. There had never been a reason to stray.

He found a card with her name on it, Angeline Bousquet; he assumed *Bousquet* was her married name. It's pretty, he thought; it suits her.

A map of the Congo was folded in a corner of the writing blotter. He spread it out on the desk. She said they were 200 kilometers northwest of Brazzaville. He measured the distance on the map with his thumb. He had been north of Loubomo, *en route* to Sibiti, when the truck was blown up. That was three days ago. The plantation was further north, in the hills between Brazzaville and Loubomo. He estimated he had traveled about fifty kilometers on foot before she found him. The rescue force should have reached the plantation by this time. It disturbed him that he could hear gun volleys and explosions; the rebels were close which must have been making the evacuation more difficult.

He lifted his eyes from the map to think. French troops were not being allowed to use force for fear of intensifying hostility and inadvertently entering into an engagement with the rebel forces. The rebels, on the other hand, were acting like aggressors and attacking the rescue forces. The Legion was being thrust into a war with their hands tied behind their back.

He looked at the map again. There were no nearby towns, savanna to the east, and an area of dense forest due west. The Gabon border was north on the other side of the hills through dense forest region. After the accident he had had the sense to head toward the hills, thinking it would be harder for the rebels to pursue him; they would stay and fight in the populated areas where they could do the most damage.

He finished with the map, folding it and making sure to place it back on the desk in the exact spot he had found it. He looked down the hallway to where she had disappeared. Her bedroom must be there, he thought. He did not want to disturb her. He went back to the kitchen for a cigarette. There was a knapsack on the counter, he wasn't sure if it had been there earlier. At some point she considered leaving on her own, he thought. He opened it up and started to go through it.

"I wanted to be prepared," she said.

The sound of her voice startled him.

"I'm sorry, I shouldn't have," he said, turning to face her. He was embarrassed to have been caught, and he smiled, the smile she already knew she loved, with his teeth showing, changing his face from brooding to irresistibly lighthearted.

"You can tell me if I packed the right things."

"It depends on what you were planning," he said.

"I wasn't sure," she said.

She was dressed in a fresh light-blue blouse that made

her eyes look more blue than green. When she stood close to him, her skin smelled of jasmine.

"You would want a water jug, a first-aid kit is always good, some penicillin, a compass. In the Legion we always have Nivaquine and salt tablets."

He saw her looking at him.

"You need a belt," she said.

She disappeared down the hallway, coming back a few minutes later with a brown leather belt folded in her hand. She looked very feminine, in a straw hat with a bell-shaped brim and a tan ribbon.

The pants stayed up with the belt, and he thanked her.

"Would you like a beer?" she asked. "Good German beer. Patrick brings it back from Europe."

She opened two bottles; the beer was not cold, but it tasted good and strong, and he drank fast. Then he began to sweat. She showed more restraint, he thought.

"I was looking for a cigarette," he said.

"I keep them hidden. It's an old habit; I used to hide them from my father after he stopped smoking."

She went and got them and they smoked and finished the beer. He could not stop from noticing her body, the breasts which showed beneath her blouse, full and soft and the curve of her hips above her thighs. Yet there was something guarded about her, something poised and cold and steady. He might have mistaken her resolve for hardness, except that she had helped him and saved his life, and so he knew she was kind beneath the aloof exterior.

"I'll show you the orchards," she said.

She saw him hesitate.

"You can look for yourself," she said, pointing toward the

veranda. "There's nothing in sight. We'll hear the rescue force coming."

The haze was blinding when they stepped outside. He shaded his eyes with his hand. The dense monotonous green was as oppressive as the light, he thought. An occasional breeze cut through the thick air, only for an instant, disappearing like sand through water.

"The coffee trees are kept at head height for harvesting," she said.

The tops were overgrown, and they walked beneath the canopy of leaves dark like laurel, with a glossy wax surface. He suddenly felt closed in, as if he were walking into an ambush. By contrast, she seemed at ease.

"Much care is taken to space the trees," she said. "You wouldn't know it because they grow so dense it's as if they'd grown wild. These are robusta trees. They are really quite hardy. They do not need shade and they can grow at lower altitudes. The trees can grow to be ten feet high, but we keep them shorter because the harvest is done by hand."

He looked up, straining to see the sky through the leaves. "How many years do you have to wait before they produce for you?" he asked.

"Five years," she said. "Then every twenty-five years the trees have to be replaced. The harvest takes place in September or October." She reached up and broke off a cluster of green-blue cherries in her hand.

"The cherries start out as bunches of white jasmine-like flowers. In the morning after it rains we wake up and find the ground covered with tiny white blossoms, like a snowstorm," she smiled to herself, not to him. "The flowers last only a few days. Like all things of beauty, they are short lived."

He tried to meet her gaze, as if to tell her he agreed—not just beauty, happiness, peace, anything good, but she did not look up at him.

Beneath the scented shade of the trees the air seemed tolerable. He followed as she walked ahead, pulling gently at the branches. It seemed she was looking for something. When she found it she stopped.

"Here," she said, holding out her hand to show him, "When they are bright red and the same shape as ordinary fruit cherries, they are considered ripe."

She gestured for him to take the smooth red fruit.

"Put it to your lips," she said. "The best way to tell when they are ripe is by the taste."

He sucked on it before opening it with his teeth. It was both sweet and bitter, he thought.

She had stopped walking and was facing him. His eyes met hers boldly, not the warm gaze that had covered her face only moments before, darker, foretelling of ecstasy and death. She was so close he could smell the jasmine on her skin. The shade of the trees cast her face in shadow, and her eyes glistened like the sunlight against the monotonous green. He put his hand to her face, and drew her to him. And in almost the same instant, as if it were a dance, she pushed him away.

He did not move, waiting for her to say something.

In a quiet voice she told him, "We should both rest," as if nothing had happened.

Then she walked on ahead of him.

Beyond the orchard, next to a large shed, there were

picked cherries in a wooden frame drying in the sun. The smell of smoke in the air overwhelmed whatever scent they might have had. He felt numb from exhaustion; it came on him suddenly.

It was quiet throughout the house. He went to the room behind the kitchen where he had spent the night. Before resting, he opened the slats of the shutters to be able to see out from bed. *Merde*, she was right; no troops, no one, nothing, he thought.

CHAPTER FIVE

When he got up it was nearly dusk and the temperature was more bearable. He had not slept more than a few minutes on and off, the rest of the time he felt sick; the air was too thick to sleep.

He found Angeline on the veranda. In the distance the surface of the forest moved like water in the last rays of slanting light. There was a weak breeze with the coming of dusk in which one could smell the bougainvillea.

"Patrick says it takes one thousand men following one leader and you could overthrow this government or any government in Africa. Do you think he's right?"

"I don't know. It depends on the determination of both sides."

She gave a slight shrug of her shoulders. "I'm not sure it matters who is in power. In the long run it amounts to the same thing."

"Why did your father stay on after independence?" he asked.

"He couldn't afford to leave. He wouldn't have been able to sell the plantation. Without it he had nothing. So he stayed. He paid what he had to—bribes to the government as well as the opposition. For as long as that went on no one bothered us."

"You're hoping this time will be the same."

She looked at him, and with her eyes she said, yes, with her pale, green, talking eyes.

Neither was very hungry. They ate on the veranda without fanfare, the remainder of the bread from the morning with cured ham. Large black flies hovered over the table. Whenever one landed, he would kill it with the back of his hand and brush it onto the ground. The others continued to hover imperviously, waiting their turn to die.

She brought out a bottle of red wine and opened it in front of him, then poured two glasses.

"It is a custom in Africa to open the bottle in front of the guest, so he can be sure it isn't poisoned," she said without irony.

"I would have trusted you."

"Because you are not African. But to survive here you must think like an African, and here there is a great fear of being poisoned."

Looking at her pretty white features and her soft mane of hair, it didn't feel like Africa, he thought, a dream, perhaps, but not Africa. Yet it puzzled him that she would take a local superstition seriously while seeming almost indifferent to the violence that threatened her.

"There is a freedom to living here. It's too soon for you to know. It takes a long time, longer than a year or two, and then you will see. "

She dipped her bread in the wine to make it soft. He was thirsty, and he drank to quench his thirst. It had been a while since he had drunk wine. In the time he had spent in Africa, it was always beer, watery and warm, or cheap whisky drunk for the sake of drinking something that might make the monotony of the heat and the poverty easier to bear.

The sun was devoured in a single gasp. Green clumps of trees turned to black; the hills in the distance appeared dark and small. The way the sun set on the equator, without warning, it was as if an unseen hand had pulled a switch, he thought. The day split between dark and light, like all the other contrasts, in stark opposition with no chance of compromise.

She ran her hands up her arms and pulled down her sleeves. The nightly torment of mosquitoes had begun with the coming of dusk. "This will help," she said, as she lit the candles on the table.

He noticed her hands in the candlelight. She had beautiful, solid hands and long slender fingers with no polish on the nails. He never liked color on a woman's hands; it reminded him of the prostitutes that were always around military bases.

The wax gave off a lavender scent as it burned, which he assumed was keeping the mosquitoes away. It did not have the same effect on the moths; they hovered so close to the flames that their wings were singed and they fell onto the table, stunned and unable to fly.

He was sweating; it was still hot, though the sun had gone down. The first glass of wine left him feeling vaguely drunk. His body was worn out by fever and exhaustion, and the wine affected him more easily. It felt good to be drunk, he thought, even the mosquitoes seemed less annoying.

"Your husband's my size," he said, pointing to the shirt he was wearing.

Her face opened up into a broad smile, "Patrick is a bigger man, over six feet. The clothes I gave you were my father's. I could not bring myself to get rid of his things when he died, anymore than I could bear the sight of some houseboy wearing one of his jackets, so I kept them."

25

Her eyes were lowered, he thought to avert his gaze, which against his will was too intense at that moment.

"And you," she asked, "Are you married?"

"No. I've never been anywhere long enough."

The night was as still as a painting; there was a mist from the humidity, and the air did not move. He kept listening for a noise, but there was only the din of insects. At times during the silence in their conversation he could hear her breathing softly.

"You were asleep in the room this morning when I woke up," he said.

"I didn't want to be alone. It felt better just to know there was someone else here."

He was struck by the honesty of her answer.

She refilled their glasses. Her voice seemed lighter to him as she spoke. He attributed it to the wine. They drank until the bottle was empty. But he was already drunk well before they had finished. He watched her profile in the candlelight, the vein that appeared in her long slender neck when she turned her head or her face in its frame of heavy dark hair. When he looked at her, the endless African landscape shrunk to nothing more than a table on a terrace where a few candles burned.

"Why have you stayed all these years?" he asked.

"I don't know how to live anywhere else," she answered.

She tilted her wine glass toward the candle, and the crystal sparkled red in the light of the flame.

"Everything I know is here," she said, "the plantation, this house. Where else in the world is there a sky as immense as this? You've noticed the sky here?"

"It's gray," he said, "more often than it's blue. It's a sad sky.

And these other things, the house, the farm, I wouldn't count on finding them when I came back. "

"You assume I'll flee," she said, calmly. "My mother fled. She hated the Congo. She blamed the tropics for my brother's death; he died of fever. I was just born and she fell into despair and gave me to an African woman to care for me. She was so hurt by my brother's death; I think she was afraid to feel after that. She went back to France. I had just turned fourteen and was in my second year at the convent school in Brazzaville. A few months later she was killed in an auto accident."

She fidgeted with her wedding band, turning it and pushing it up and down her finger. She would not lift her eyes as she spoke.

"I tried to pack a valise this afternoon. I didn't know what to take or where I would go. I remembered going to Paris for my mother's funeral, the way it rained on and off, without ever clearing up, and the damp chill through my coat. My father asked me if I wanted to stay with my aunt. He told me France was a wonderful place for a little girl to grow up. I came back to Africa with him. I am not the kind of person who leaves."

He suddenly understood the expression he had seen on her face during the day which had baffled him, the reason why her eyes did not blink at the sound of the gunfire, why she did not look over her shoulder when they were walking through the orchard or why she had seemed so detached when he spoke of the rescue force.

"We're entering the dry season; it will be too hot, unbearable. Everyone will retreat to the shade wherever they can find it and the fighting will stop."

She was wrong, he thought. "You can't stay here. It's not safe." His tone left no room for doubt.

"You wouldn't understand. Patrick will be back soon. It doesn't matter if the borders are closed. He was born here; he knows how to get things done. We will manage."

"You think a few bribes will make it right. If your husband doesn't come back with an army, he won't be able to help you. The rebels are out of control." He was drunk and he spoke without inhibition, whereas earlier he had held back. "You think you can stay here. Dogs and birds—that's what's thriving here now. In less than a week Brazzaville has been destroyed; the buildings are burnt out, there's shattered glass all over, as if it had rained glass. They're pouring gasoline on white people and burning them. Do you know what burning flesh smells like? What would it take? A white woman alone—five minutes to half an hour to kill you, depending on whether they bothered to rape you while you were still alive."

"You were there and you did nothing to stop it."

"Those were my orders. Condemn me if you like."

He heard the wine in his voice; he sounded arrogant and defensive at the same time. It had not been easy to watch and do nothing.

"You want to believe the violence is random," he said. "In Brazzaville they jeered and spat at us and called us names because we were white. You are a *colon*. Hatred for you is in their blood; it never dies, maybe it goes away for a time, goes into remission like a cancer, but it never dies, not until all the *colons* are gone. They want Africa for themselves."

She clenched her hands around her glass; her lower lip seemed to tremble. "You don't know what you're saying. You haven't lived here. You weren't born here. Don't you think Africa is in my blood too? Why does it have to be about color?"

"Because it is."

Something told him he should stop. Maybe it was the wine, but he could not stop.

"You can't pretend anymore," he said. "Your fairy-tale Africa, the blue sky paradise doesn't exist anymore. You can't hide in your *colon's* house with its white walls and long windows and think you can beat everything around you into submission the way the big fans on your ceiling beat the stifling air into a breeze. You can't live surrounded by poverty, hunger and ignorance and think somehow you will go unscathed."

"It was you who did nothing when they threw the man over the bridge."

She banged her glass and it fell over, the last sips of wine spilling like blood across the linen napkin. He reached to pick up the glass; to his surprise it had not broken. He set it upright.

"Yet you would condemn me," she said.

"No," he shook his head and tried to take her hand but she pulled back. "I am not condemning you; I want you to understand you can't stay here anymore. They will kill you."

Through the candle's flame he felt her eyes staring angrily back at him. When he looked up she had turned her gaze to somewhere beyond him, to her trees with their white scented flowers which fell like snow on the warm ground. Suddenly he felt as if he were intruding, as if he should not be there.

"And when they do kill me, will you stand there and watch? Those are your orders, aren't they?"

She got up and went inside. And then the night that only

moments before had seemed to stop at the other end of the table was once more immense and foreboding, and the loneliness he felt brought him to his feet and caused him to seek solace inside the walls of his room.

He saw the knapsack in the kitchen. Whatever was in there was better than nothing, and he thought he should keep it within reach during the night, so he brought it with him.

He lay down, placing the Beretta on his stomach where he knew he could find it in a hurry if he had to. His body sank into the soft bed.

He had not meant to upset her that way. He should have been more sensitive to what she was being asked to give up. The wine clouded his thoughts; he was tired too. In the morning he would apologize. His thoughts went back to the day in the jeep. Why was there no rescue? Reinforcements never arrived, though they radioed for them. How had he awakened hours later, the dead body on top of him, hard and cold and heavy as stone?

He closed his eyes; the night noises made a rhythm in his head. A moment later he was asleep.

Angeline did not sleep. She lit a cigarette from the citronella candle burning at her bedside and pushed back the mosquito netting draped like a canopy from above her bed. "My little bird in her cage," Patrick would say when he came into the room and she was in bed. It seemed safer, more protected, to be a bird in a cage. Though she never minded when Patrick was gone; it suited her independence.

She smoked slowly. She was uncertain of the time, but it was not late, certainly before ten. It was only because she had been upset that she had gone inside.

She knew it was more than what the soldier had said about not being able to remain in the Congo that had upset her. In the orchard when he tried to kiss her, though she refused, that brief exchange had drawn them closer, forcing her to acknowledge to herself, at least, the desire she had been feeling.

The cigarette was hot against her fingers; lost in thought, the plantation, the rebels, the soldier, the same round of images going over in her head until they all seemed to be one, she had smoked to the end of the cigarette without noticing. There was a sudden noise, a branch cracking. She sat upright and listened. Then nothing. The night noises she had always known, the insomnia of the Congo, the rustling of animals in the trees, the ebb and flow of insect noises. Outside the night presented a still face, and the darkness seemed so close, pressing up against the window. She listened for a long time until, still dressed, she dozed off.

CHAPTER SIX

He had slept for a little over three hours when he was awakened by the sound of glass breaking followed by an explosion. He heard his heart pounding in his chest and in the split second between waking and sleep, he thought he had been blown up. His arm clutched reflexively at the gun on his stomach. He did not turn on the light, but a quick glance told him there was no one in the room; the sound had come from somewhere else in the house.

He grabbed the pile of clothes from the chair and slipped the knapsack over his shoulder as he went out into the hall. He could smell the smoke. Someone hurled a torch through the broken doors. There was a second explosion at the end of the house where he had been sleeping. The air was turning hot, and he heard the sound of the walls cracking, giving in to the heat and flames. Keeping his head low, he made his way through the smoke filled hallway. He tripped over a step at the entrance to the hall where her bedroom was, but caught his balance without falling.

"Angeline," he called out, not sure which room was hers. He held his gun, ready to shoot, as he opened the door. There was no one. He moved quickly down the hall. He could hear shouting coming from another part of the house. He kicked open the door. She was on the bed, clutching a gun with both hands, her eyes wide and round. She seemed too frightened to move.

He went to the window. They'd go out through there, he thought, lifting a slat with his finger and looking outside. It seemed that whoever was attacking was on the other side of the house.

He dressed quickly. When he looked up, she was still clutching the gun.

"Go out the window," he said. Then he noticed she was barefoot. "Where are your shoes? You need shoes."

She just stood there staring mutely back at him like a frightened animal. Not wanting to waste any more time, he reached his hand under the bed and fumbled in the dark. He felt the room getting hot and a burst of light. There was a loud noise. In that moment, a gun fired, and through the smoke and the darkness he saw a body fall forward to the ground.

"Just go." He felt the frenzy in his voice; he was not sure whether he was shouting. "Go, go, through the window, start running."

He kept his eyes and gun pointed at the door. At the sound of the gunshot, other guns began firing into empty rooms. A shining black pool of blood was oozing across the floor.

She remained staring at the fallen body, the gun hanging from her hand. He grabbed her arm and held her tightly, too tightly; he thought he might have hurt her.

"Go, now. There's no time," he shouted as he dragged her to the window.

There must have been flames in the hall because he could

hear the voices, but no one came right away, not until they were both out the window.

The flames were shooting through the roof of the house. He saw her watching the house as it burned. She began to cry. He took her hand and pulled her.

"We have to run. We will die here."

They headed toward the coffee orchards. As they passed the first shed an arm the color of the night lunged out from behind the shed and grabbed her.

Vincent pointed his gun.

Someone slightly older than a boy had wrapped his arm around Angeline's neck and was covering her mouth while pointing a *Kalishnikov* at Vincent from close enough range to blow off his face.

"Madame Angeline," he said in a hushed voice. "It's me, Ahmed. They are going to burn the trees. Go away from the farm into the hills."

He let her go.

"Thank you, Ahmed," she said in a whisper.

"Madame Angeline, you will not tell anyone?"

"No, Ahmed, I promise."

Ahmed fired his gun into the night in the opposite direction.

"Stay low," Vincent told her as they ran. This was an untrained army. The soldiers did not know how to keep their aim. He believed for as long as they kept moving and crouched low enough they would make it.

They ran half a kilometer until they reached a few scattered trees with trunks big enough to hide behind.

He waited for her to catch her breath.

"Who is Ahmed?"

"He has worked for me since he was a child. His father worked for my father."

"Now he is burning his livelihood," Vincent said, though she did not answer him.

They rested without speaking a few minutes longer. She pressed her face against her knees as she sat.

"Can you continue?" he asked.

She nodded, getting up.

They could see the flames. The trees were burning in the still night. Vincent faulted himself for looking out all evening into that menacing stillness and not having anticipated the attack, for allowing himself to be lulled into the belief that they could afford to wait. His whole life waiting had brought nothing.

He saw her look back in the direction of the house.

"It's all burning," she said.

"Don't look," he said, putting his arms around her. Yellow streaks of fire streamed upward into the black night.

"Nothing will be left," she said, "only the stone walls, the iron balustrade. . . . It's too late." She hid her face in his chest.

There was another explosion, and he felt the tremor of her body against his. They were still too close to the danger. The fire was burning around them. He knew they had to continue, but in what direction?

As if she could read his thoughts, "This is the right way," she said. "Across the hills. It will be safe there."

She seemed sure, and he deferred to her and kept going.

The terrain began to slope upward. He felt as if the hills had closed around them. Everywhere was pitch black.

He went a few steps further before he realized she was not behind him.

"Angeline," he called out her name. He heard her answer, though he groped in the dark before he found her.

He knelt beside her and spoke in a gentle voice. "We have to keep going."

Her voice sounded weak. "I hurt my foot," she said. "I can't walk on it. I can't go any further tonight," she said.

He put his hand to her foot; the skin was swollen and moist with blood. He reached into the knapsack, grateful for having had the presence of mind to keep it with him, and fumbled through the contents until he came across the bottle of alcohol.

"It will sting," he said as he poured it over the swollen area.

She let out a gasp. Her eyes glistened and he took that to be tears. He tore off the end of his sleeve and wrapped it around her foot.

"We have to keep going. They'll find us here; we are too close. It will be easier if I carry you on my back."

She put her arms around his neck and rested her head against his shoulder.

"When we reach the top we can rest. It's enough of a head start in the morning," he said.

It seemed she was already very far away.

The crows cawed and screeched from the branches of the trees. Their wings flapped loudly in the restless dawn. There were birds with red crowns; he did not know the name. He thought, too many birds to know the names of each kind, if there even was a name. Enough to know that its song was sad.

Ashes from the fire had fallen like snow through the night, long, thin black ashes. Ordinarily dawn came suddenly, from dark to light, like the opening of an eye after a night's sleep. But because of the fire the sky was laden with smoke and the night hovered like a cloud. He stretched out his legs. The adrenaline was gone and he felt exhausted.

She was asleep on her left side. This was good, he thought, because of the swelling in her foot. He had been proved right; she could not have stayed in that house. Yet he felt no satisfaction. He felt sorry for her. He was a child when he learned what it was to lose everything. There were no words for that. He remembered his mother's face when he was brought to see her for the last time. Her eyes were glistening, but the tears were his; she was too sick. The dying have nothing left for tears; it is the living who cry.

CHAPTER SEVEN

When she awoke she was alone. It was daylight though the sky was black.

"Vincent," she called out his name, quietly, yet with desperation, believing he was gone. Her foot hurt badly, and she undid the bandage. The skin was swollen and red. In the light she could see the two fang marks where the snake had bitten her. She took the bandage and wrapped it above her knee to prevent the venom from traveling.

A bird was singing in the branches above her, a syrupy song, as she lay back down in the wet, black grass, too weak to stand. In which direction should she go anyway? Smoke hung in a dark cloud over the hills. A chill came over her suddenly, and she wanted to be covered, a blanket, anything— worst of all was to lie there exposed.

Was it finished? The fire? The rebels? And if it were finished, when would it be safe to go back? Watching the smoke hang like a thick curtain, she wondered why the sun, stronger than anything in Africa, had not burned through the clouds. The fire must still be burning, she thought.

She remembered being awakened by a loud noise and reaching into the drawer of her bed stand for the revolver and the twenty thousand francs. It seemed it was at that moment that the French soldier came into the room, imploring her to leave. She pictured the image of his pale silhouette in the doorway. She thought, he has come to save me. Tell him I don't want to be saved. I want to die, here, now. He said they had to run. She had been waiting, though she did not know what she was waiting for until later, when the door opened a second time. In the light of the fire, she saw the cruel, disturbed look of the man's face. She shot without thinking, the way a trapped animal pounces first, and only after, in the spray of blood like warm, sweet rain, did she realize what she had done.

In her mind she saw the blackened walls of the house, flames spiraling through every room, turning everything to ashes, and with it the dead body of the man she had shot— the image that had been missing.

The bird was staring at her too intently. She knew its song now, not sleep, but death, the intoxicating invitation. She shut her eyes. The bamboos burned like grass and made a creaking sound like a cry of pain. They are grass, not trees, hollow on the inside, her father had told her when she was a little girl. They were burning very hot and bright like slender candles on top of a birthday cake. And the other trees, fern trees and phantom palms and perfume trees—a name she made up herself when she was a child because the tree was fragrant and sweet like a flower and always filled with large red ants—they were burning straight up. The coffee trees were too close together. They burned in rows. The photograph of her mother and father and Joachim burned from the edges—when it was finished who would remember they were smiling?

It was hot and still and dry despite the dark sky. The bird

with the glassy eye and the sweet voice was lulling her, and memory was nothing compared with the dream that was sleep itself. She was only half aware of Vincent as he bent down beside her. He opened his hands and out flew a red butterfly that fluttered near their faces before escaping into the air.

"I thought you had gone," she said. Her face, which yesterday had seemed so still, now seemed to quiver, and her eyes had a remote look, not dazed or panicked, but sleepy like her voice.

The bird stopped singing and flew out of the branches.

"I went to look for water." He stroked her hand soothingly. "Let me see your foot," he said.

"A snakebite," she said.

He looked at her for an instant, his gaze meeting hers; the stakes had changed again. They both knew it.

"I think it was a bush viper. Whatever it was, it had to have been a small snake."

He gently touched the bruised, swollen skin and it opened with puss. Tearing off the other end of his shirtsleeve, he wrapped it around her foot. There could be leopards in the hills and they would pick up the scent of blood.

It was a lousy thing to have happened, he thought. He touched her forehead, "You don't have a fever," he said. "Lie on your left side for now. It's best to be immobile."

She gazed up at him. "I didn't mean to kill him. I saw his face in the doorway and before I knew what I was doing I fired."

"You were right to shoot him," he said. "He would have killed you. Did you know him?"

"I didn't recognize him at first, not until this morning

when I thought about it. His name is Oman. He comes down from the Angola border where the rebels train their armies. He came to Patrick threatening to cause trouble if he were not paid."

"What did Patrick do?"

"He refused."

"So he came back last night."

He was silent for a moment. "We have to keep going," he said. "It's not good to stay in the same place for too long, and you need treatment. Do you know where we are?"

She nodded, "To the north," she said, "on the other side of the hills, near the entrance to the forest, there is a village; Marguerite, who took care of me when I was a child, lives not far from there. She will not turn us away."

The haze was clearing and he could see green below, which meant there must be water.

"Do you know the way?" he asked. He felt the thirst burning against the back of his throat, another measure of time running out.

"We have to go through the hills heading due west. It's not hard; it will just take time."

He looked down at her foot as if to calculate how much time they had.

"We will get there in time," she said.

"What about the Gabon border? We're close aren't we?" He was thinking ahead to the next step, after they got help for her.

"Marguerite is a *féticheuse*. People come to her. She will know where the rebels are hiding."

He knew Africans enlisted the help of the *féticheuse* when they were sick or had a dispute they wanted resolved in their favor. The *féticheuse* was believed to have special powers of magic and clairvoyance.

She made an effort to walk, but it was too hard, and he wrapped his arm across her back to support her.

The sky was white, not blue, the haze blinding and the air thick. He noticed she was adjusted to the climate and to the terrain; it did not waste her the way it might have someone who had not lived there her whole life. But she was ill and they were a long time without anything to drink.

In the distance he saw a slender brown form walking with a large sack on his back, a man traveling alone. He was too far away to be a threat. It was like that in Africa. His company would be out on a field sortie in the middle of nowhere when a local would emerge walking insouciantly in the grueling heat, headed who knows where, as if he were out for an afternoon stroll.

From the top of the hill they could see bright green trees and, in a clearing, the straw tops of houses, some rounded, others pointed.

"The huts are made of mud and grass mixed with scraps of tin and iron, and when it rains they leak," she said. "Each year after the rainy season, they have to be rebuilt."

He was beginning to understand; nothing here was meant to last, only the bush and the immense sky with its rolling black clouds and its burning sun.

Closer to the bottom they heard a screeching noise.

"The monkeys are fighting," she said.

It was an awful sound, he thought.

A dirt path between the trees led to a narrow river; the water was brown and seemingly still. He knew the surface appeared calm, but below the current was strong.

It was not only the river that could deceive; the forest, which had appeared ordinary at first, was in fact menacing. Enormous ferns, wide as an elephant's ear, made it difficult to find a path for walking. The reeds were sharp and cut their legs with long fine scratches. There were flamingos fishing off the riverbanks, belonging more to her world of magic than to any world that he recognized.

They came to a narrow bridge made of woven grass and suspended from a tree on each bank. It hung not quite two meters above the water and was barely wide enough to fit one person at a time. But she could not walk without his help. He carried her on his back, hoping the bridge could withstand their weight.

"It isn't far," she said as if to reassure him.

"Isn't she afraid to live here by herself?" he asked.

She smiled, the first time he had seen her smile since that first morning. "It's said even the evil spirits are afraid of her. The people in the village tell a story about a man who came to her with a chicken, and in front of her he cut the chicken in half; Marguerite sprinkled water on the two halves and they joined together again and the chicken got up and ran away."

"It's a trick," he said.

"Soon you will meet her and you will judge for yourself," she answered.

CHAPTER EIGHT

They reached Marguerite at dusk. In the dying light they saw her standing outside her hut made of wood with a thatched roof. A small patch of cassava grew in front of the hut and a chicken ran in the dirt.

"*Ma biche,*" my doe, she said, fixing her eyes on Angeline. Marguerite took Angeline's hair in her hands and let it shroud her shoulders as she held her. In Marguerite's arms Angeline began to sob, as if she had been waiting, holding it inside all the while. Marguerite whispered, "I know, *ma biche,* I know what they do," speaking as if Vincent were not there, a soft, lulling whisper as one might use in consoling a crying child. And seeing her in the *féticheuse's* arms, Vincent thought, she is more African than I saw at first, despite her light hair and light eyes.

Marguerite was tall and thin. The yellow-green scarf wound high on her head made her appear even taller. A necklace of shells of different sizes hung around her neck. It made no noise when she moved, so precise were her movements. He was struck at once by her large, sunken eyes against her dark skin, skin black as night with a purple luster. (Here when a woman's skin is very dark, the men believe she is possessed by a demon or spirit and fear her. He had heard that somewhere. In Djibouti the girls bleached their skin with hydroquinone.)

When she at last let her gaze shift in his direction, it was to give him a hard, accusatory stare.

Vincent had never seen such a still face; nothing moved when she spoke. Her large eyes on the still gaunt face gave the impression of a spirit inhabiting a corpse.

She told them to come in. As she walked, the tops of her dry, gray feet peeked out of the long cotton shift that she wore like a ceremonial robe as it dragged along the dirt floor of the hut. The incongruity between the hut and the objects inside struck Vincent immediately. There was French and Italian faience, bowls and pitchers with blue and yellow designs, set out on a small mahogany commode. Copper pots hung from a rod in the mud wall. A French toile curtain divided the room in two. On the other side, the thin mattress where Marguerite slept was covered with white, stiff sheets. There were two wooden chairs that looked as if they had come from a church in Provence, and worn paisley cushions in a neat pile.

Marguerite looked over toward Vincent, coldly, knowingly. "Tell the French soldier be careful not to speak too loud in the forest. The spirits listen," she said.

"I have said nothing," he said, annoyed, but it was as if she had read his mind.

She answered, "The spirits hear with their eyes too."

She gave them each a cup of cool water.

"You sick, *ma biche*. I see your foot."

"She's been bitten by a snake. She needs antivenom," though after saying it, he realized at once the futility of the statement.

Marguerite said to Angeline, "You come with me now,"

her voice full of command, as if with each word she were rendering a verdict.

She put her arm around Angeline as she took her behind the curtain. Angeline acquiesced, seeming docile and obedient like a dutiful child. It annoyed him to see her that way.

He listened closely, but could make out nothing, only the rustle of clothes. Then he heard her, Marguerite, the slow, steady *patois*, low and soft and indiscernible.

"Bush snake," Marguerite said, holding Angeline's foot and examining it under the light of a candle. "They don't kill you."

Angeline could feel the heat of the flame.

Marguerite rubbed the area with a sponge soaked in whisky. When the burning stopped, she mixed a white powder with water and let it dry in a paste over the bruise. Angeline felt the skin stiffening beneath it as it dried.

Marguerite said, "Strong at first for white skin, but it works just the same black or white." She put her hands on Angeline's arms. "The mosquitoes feast on you last night. My salve works there too." Then she covered the bites with the white mixture.

"They burn your house, your plantation, all your possessions to the ground. They are drunk with evil and destroying. It makes my heart hurt to think what they do to you. This much I know: they don't try this if your father were alive. He stop them good."

Angeline knew Marguerite faulted Patrick for leaving her alone so often.

"I do what I can. I take care of your foot first, then I wash the ashes from your skin so nothing left for the spirits to smell. When you clean, I give you something make you sleep deep and sound like death."

Angeline watched her moving about the room, knowing every movement, every gesture she made was necessary, nothing wasted—the wave of her hand, even the whisper of air around her long skirt shunning the spirit of evil that was always watching, listening. The flame wavered and flickered and the shadows grew long and sharp like knives against the side of the hut and across the ceiling before the flame burst and extinguished suddenly. She shuddered.

"How the French soldier comes to you?" Marguerite asked.

"I found him in the grass outside the orchard. He had a fever and I helped him."

"It's his time to die when you find him. You do wrong to save him. I feel the death chill in my bones when I see him, so I know what I say is right."

Marguerite shook her head. "No happiness comes to the French soldier. I know because I see in his eyes—when the white shows below the pupil the spirits mark him for sadness. You feel weak for his handsome face. The woman who loves him cries long and hard in the night. The spirits give him such a handsome face to make it all the more pitiful when they destroy him."

She rested her hand on Angeline's shoulder. "You feel for him, *hein*. You don't give in yet, I see that too. If tomorrow you love him, you cry yourself to death. Forget what you feel for him. You ask my advice, that's what I tell you."

Angeline thought of the day in the orchard when he

tried to kiss her and how she desired him then. Yet she had stopped him, prevented things from going any further. She knew she could not walk away from him the way one must be able to walk away in the tropics to avoid going mad.

"Then I will stay with you. He can go on without me; it will be better for him too."

"You stay with me more than one night, they find you here. My power has limits. I am no sorcerer. Tonight you sleep. You go when you wake. Let the French soldier take you to a safe place. He has a good heart to go with his handsome face."

Marguerite stroked Angeline's hair before giving her something to drink, white and cloudy like milk.

"I make *nkisi* for you like when you a child. You right to be afraid, but the nail fetish I make for you chase the fear away," she said, holding the disfigured little nail in her palm for Angeline to see.

It was after her mother had died. She did not return to school at once, but stayed at the house with her father and Marguerite. At night she was awakened by dreams. She still believed in heaven, and the dream was always the same, her mother in heaven that appeared in the dream as an enormous forest, and her mother looked hurt and lost. Marguerite gave her the *nkisi* and told her to press down on it when the dream woke her. And it was true, the dream went away for the night, at least, and she could go back to sleep.

A mattress rested on a narrow metal frame a few inches above the ground.

Marguerite took Angeline's clothes. "You sleep better when you are cool," she said.

After she had undressed she saw Vincent through the opening in the curtain. His gaze sought out hers, looking at her through brooding gray eyes. She crossed her hands over her breasts to cover herself and looked away.

When Marguerite put her hand to her face to embrace her, she touched tears.

"Cry, *ma biche*, cry, a little longer, cry 'til you sleep, deep like death, and you forget."

CHAPTER NINE

It was hot and airless in the hut.

Marguerite appeared from behind the curtain and sat over a small cooking fire stirring something in a pot. *Fou-fou*, she called it when she put down the bowl in front of Vincent with a small carafe of palm wine. The food was heavily spiced which made it palatable.

He went outside. It was already dark. The moon filtered through the trees in silver streaks. There was the racket of insects and bats beating their wings in the branches above. He felt ill and hopeless. He doubted whether the *féticheuse* could do anything to help Angeline. They needed a doctor, a Red Cross station; she could die without proper treatment.

The night noises made a sound like an iron chain being dropped against a hard floor, the menacing chant of some breed of cricket or locust, unbroken like the night itself, a prison without a window out. And always, always the stifling heat—then why in all this heat was he shivering? His body heaved and a thin sweet saliva filled his mouth until a terrible cramp caused him to double over and vomit.

☙

"You sleep beneath the tree all night, the witches see you spy on them and they make trouble," Marguerite said.

He had slept all night beneath the tree—past the first light and the first cries of the birds. He felt his head throbbing and his throat was sore from thirst.

"Where is Angeline?"

"You protect her, French Soldier. I already protect her, but what I do is not enough."

He went behind the curtain to look for her. She was asleep, if he could call it sleep; her hair was wet with sweat and her skin was sallow and ashen as if she were dead. He went closer and held her wrist in his hand, feeling the weak pulse.

He heard Marguerite behind him.

"What I give her make her sleep."

"She's sleeping too deeply," he said, still holding Angeline's limp wrist in his hand.

"She wake up soon enough. Recovered too," she said as she glared at him with her hostile eyes. The eyes of a carrion bird, he thought. She was so close he could see tiny bubbles of saliva at the corners of her dry mouth.

"She needs a doctor," he said.

"I know better than any doctor what she needs."

"So you say. What did you give me last night to make me sick?"

She laughed aloud, a spiteful, mocking little laugh. "What you suffer you suffer from the fever; *la palu*, it never leaves—once inside you, it always comes back. The fever is like that."

Paludisme, palu, malaria—at the mention of the word he felt his shirt sticking to his back. But he recognized she was trying to make him defensive, and he would not let her. He was still holding Angeline's wrist, feeling the pulse beating steadily but weakly, counting the beats in his head. He placed her arm gently at her side and pulled the sheet up to cover her.

"Can I get to the Gabon border from here?" In his view it was the quickest way to safety.

Marguerite nodded her head up and down like a doll. "You a stranger here. The minute you forget, machete cut off your face."

Machete cut off your face. He could hear the cadence of her choppy French resounding in his head.

"Machetes with nails along the edges, I know," he said.

She bobbed her narrow head up and down. Her eyelids were nearly closed.

"I see what I see," she said. "The dead man's spirit lead them to her. I try to protect her. He torment them until they find her. I know who they are, but what I do is not enough. I cannot make people live or die."

"You think this mob of lunatics will be organized enough to seek her out?"

"*Je sais ce que je sais.*"

Rays of sunlight burst through the openings in the shutter.

"You still have not told me whether I can get to Gabon from here." He was losing patience with the conversation. "Is there a map?" he asked.

"Once a year I take the ferry to Impfondo; for that I don't need a map."

The hut was airless and he had the feeling of suffocating. He saw her studying him attentively.

"Do you believe in God, French Soldier? I see in your eyes, you believe. Here a person has to believe in God for living same as dying, no difference."

He watched Angeline's chest rise in her sleep with each breath, God, he thought, why not God?

"She wake up soon. She sleep until the poison gone from her."

There was no use staying inside the hut. He felt his head throbbing and the ache in his legs and he went out again.

He did not know how long he had been sitting there before Marguerite came out.

"Drink my coffee and see how it clears your head."

The coffee was strong and hot and he felt the sweat dripping down his back.

"You perspire," Marguerite said. "White people come here and they don't sweat; the climate too much for their white skin."

He did not look up or meet her eyes. The chickens were making a racket in the coop and there was the sound of the *féticheuse's* skirt flapping against the dirt like a flag in the wind.

"Where can I get water to wash?" he asked.

Marguerite directed him to the river. "You take this," she said, handing him a large, yellow plastic container.

Wrapping a white cloth around his head to prevent his scalp from burning in the sun, he headed out. The river was not far; he found it easily—a crystalline gap in the grass and trees. Water flowed down the rocks into a bathing pool and made a mist in the heat. The grass was soft and short, and the air had the strong sweet scent of the lilies that grew wild nearby.

He filled the water jar. Then he undressed and bathed. The water was cool and it felt good. He looked up between the spaces of the trees at the sky which was blue, a deep blue, so deep he could see traces of gray.

He noticed a monkey staring at him from the low branch of a tree. Its eyes so still and fixed startled him at first. When he saw it was only a monkey, he grinned, and the monkey screeched back at him.

A short while later a group of village women and girls emerged along the embankment. They just stood there holding their plastic containers as if they were waiting for something. He remembered the girl with the grenade. In appearance she was no different than these girls. Then it occurred to him that they were waiting for him to leave before filling their water containers.

He got out of the water and dressed and started back along the narrow pathway beaten into the forest.

Out of the trees and toward the clearing he could see a black cloud of smoke to the west that meant the fighting was still going on, though overhead the sky was blue. He thought of Angeline; this was the blue sky she had been referring to, blue and immense, when she asked him if he had noticed the sky. Here there was nothing but open sky. But less than thirty feet from where he was standing it was tropical forest.

It was the desolation of extremes existing side by side, the heat of the day against the chill of the night, the hill springing suddenly out of the plateau, that gave him the sense of being always off balance, that it was a wild place and there were no rules.

As he approached, he saw Marguerite sitting beneath the shade of a tree as if she owned the world. To his surprise, Angeline was sitting beside her. Her hair was combed back off her face and hung to her waist. Marguerite was brushing it. He could see the red and gold lights in it. She appeared different to him, as if he were seeing her for the first time. She no longer belonged to the plantation where she had spent her life; there was nowhere she belonged now, and in this she was like him, he thought.

Marguerite took the water from him without a word and went into the hut.

"I am sorry Marguerite was harsh with you," Angeline said. "She never doubts herself, and she is not afraid to say what she thinks."

"You seem better. I'm grateful to her for that."

Not only her foot, everything about her seemed better; her eyes were soft and shining in the daylight and there was color in her face.

"She is cold to strangers, cold and distrusting. It's so she can protect herself. To her a stranger can be the bearer of an evil spirit or the devil himself."

"She told you I was the Devil? You don't believe in any of that?" he said, amused.

"She doesn't think you're the Devil."

"I saw you this morning; I wasn't sure you'd wake up. She drugged you, didn't she?"

"She gave me something to sleep. When I was a child, it was always Marguerite who put me to sleep."

He watched her face streaked by sunlight, her eyes open and staring back at him.

"My mother was always a fragment of a story, like the petal that falls from the flower, never the rose itself. I remember that she was sad and hurt and unhappy. If there were something more, I never knew. It is different with Marguerite; she belongs here."

Marguerite prepared a feast of hard-boiled eggs and bananas and cassava dipped in caramelized sugar that was waiting for them in the hut, but she did not stay to join them.

Angeline peeled a hard-boiled egg.

"Is there a reason your Marguerite will not eat with us?" he asked.

"She eats only once a day, at four in the afternoon, always alone; it has always been that way."

"Where is she going?" She had a calico-colored scarf wound tight around her head and a large bowl balanced on top so her arms were free.

"I gave her money to buy penicillin and quinine. She knows someone who works in the infirmary; he hoards it so he can sell it."

"You trust her too much," he said.

She pushed the hair from her face, looking at him through heavy eyelids that shaded her pale eyes. "We cannot go through Gabon; the rebels have closed off the border. We have to go to Pointe-Noire."

"Gabon is less than fifty kilometers from here. It's the closest way out."

"Distance means nothing here—the closest place might be unreachable—it's a question of what is possible. Their camps are well known. We have to go through the interior to Pointe-Noire; there is no choice."

He got up and paced around the hut.

"The rebels have checkpoints on all the roads," she said.

"What happened to the *goddamn army* in this country?" He banged his hand against the shutter, and it swung open.

"The army is Communist, badly trained, uneducated, unmotivated because they haven't been paid in months. You saw what little use they were in Brazzaville."

"What about transportation?" he said. "Can your Marguerite get beyond the superstition to something useful, or will she blink and we'll wake up in Pointe-Noire?"

"There might not be a need for superstition in other places—here it is an answer to the questions that begin with *why.*"

"You're wrong," he said, "arbitrariness and cruelty exist everywhere."

He was sweating. He suddenly felt hot, and the air in the hut seemed so close he could not breathe. He saw the beads of sweat on her brow.

"Marguerite will talk to the chief in the village. I gave her money to arrange a ride out of the area."

"We're 300 kilometers from Pointe-Noire. How far do you think a truck could travel at night?"

She shrugged her shoulders. "No roads, in the pitch dark, fifty kilometers would be a lot. It's dangerous to drive at night; they will be afraid of ambushes and not want to go far."

A large fly alighted on his face. He chased it with the back of his hand. A minute later it was back. This time he killed it; it made a noise when it fell to the ground.

He squinted into the bright sun as he looked through the slats in the door to the outside. They didn't even have a hat between them. How could they possibly embark on a journey like this?

CHAPTER TEN

When Marguerite returned, the large bowl she had carried on her head was full.

"The truck takes you tonight. Not far, I know. The French soldier takes you the rest of the way. I give them two thousand francs for the truck," she said, handing Angeline a small purse.

Vincent looked over at Angeline as if to ask her where the money had come from.

She reached inside and took out another thousand francs and tried to give it to Marguerite.

Marguerite pushed her hand away. "Not for money I do what I do."

"What if I never see you again?" she said quietly.

"Come close. Let me look good at you," she said pressing her withered fingers to Angeline's face and gazing straight into her eyes.

"You reach Pointe-Noire," she said wistfully. Her tone changed; she seemed cold and certain. "Tell the French soldier I bring him a present. A razor to shave his face."

Marguerite filled the knapsack with the things she had brought from the village, manioc flour, sugar, coffee, biscuits, a carefully folded *moustiquaire*, a plastic tarp, as well as mosquito repellant and a vial with a few penicillin pills.

"Tell me what you think," Angeline said, turning to Vincent, just as she had at her house that morning (or was it afternoon? he was no longer sure).

Vincent pulled out a small steel coffee pot with a porcelain handle, like the one Angeline had used to make coffee that first morning.

"We can't be bogged down carrying things like this," he said, holding out the coffee pot.

"I gave it to her as a present; she insists I take it."

"We will not be able to make it through the jungle without a machete," he said.

Marguerite answered, "I live here all my life, never outside Congo. I know what you need before you do. I give you my machete."

They heard a voice outside, a child's voice, high and plaintive. Through the shutter they saw a girl with long, thin legs like an antelope carrying a sleeping child across her arms.

"You go behind the curtain," Marguerite told them, handing Angeline the knapsack to take with her. "You being here is nobody's business."

She opened the shutter and went outside to greet the girl, taking the child in her arms.

"His arm is swollen where the mosquito bit him," the girl said in a frightened way. "*Maman* told me to bring him."

Marguerite put her fingers along the swollen forearm; the skin was purplish and it turned a reddish hue where she touched.

"He cries and cries, then he sleeps all the time. Bad sleep—he cries in his sleep."

Marguerite said nothing as the girl spoke; she did not take her eyes off the boy's arm. She carried him inside and put him down on the small table. Vincent watched through the slight gap between the wall and the curtain. Marguerite filled a tin cup with tree sap that she warmed with a match before applying it to the boy's arm. She repeated this several times, the whole procedure taking roughly twenty minutes, during which time the little boy never moved and his sister watched with wide, frightened eyes. At one point, the little girl looked up at the curtain as if she could see through it, and Vincent had the impression she knew they were there.

Marguerite stroked the sleeping boy's head before cutting a piece of his hair. The boy opened his eyes and moaned.

"Tell your mother, you bring him back tomorrow if he is still sleeping."

The girl nodded.

"You take him home now," she said. The girl lifted him and carried him on her back this time, his tiny little frame limp like a doll's.

After they had gone, Marguerite put the hair in a tin cup lined on the bottom with wax.

"For what reason did she take a cut of his hair?" Vincent asked in a low voice.

"So she can continue to treat him after he goes. Finger nail clippings, hair shavings—whatever she does to the hair she does to him."

Vincent made no comment; he was wondering whether it was sleeping sickness or malaria, whether the boy would live or die.

"They come to her complaining of insect bites, spoilt food, colic, and she heals them," she said. "Not always, but most of the time."

"When she does not?"

"Then they believe a sorcerer has cast a spell too powerful to break, and they try to find out who among their acquaintances had cast such a spell."

He watched through the opening in the curtain as the girl walked off carrying her brother into the widely spaced trees; he was now awake enough to hold on to her.

It was dusk. Above them there was an abrupt noise as a parrot flew out of the branches of a nearby tree.

"What else, Angeline? What else did Marguerite tell you last night after I left?"

It was a good minute before she answered him.

"She warned me not to fall in love with you."

"What reason did she give you?" he asked, gently.

Angeline shook her head, "I won't tell you that. Ask me anything else."

"Did you believe her? And will you do as she says?"

"They are different things. I can believe her, and not be able to change what happens."

He felt the urge to kiss her, to throw her on the ground and feel her beneath him, but he remembered what happened in the orchard (could it have been only the day before last?) and he resisted.

"Cry first because crying eases the heart, then after you sleep," she said.

He sat on the edge of the bed and touched her hair, " "Did you cry?"

"Last night, yes."

CHAPTER ELEVEN

"Vincent," Angeline called gently to wake him, "They will be here soon."

She knelt so close he could smell the jasmine on her skin.

"It's going to go all right," he said.

That hour's sleep had been necessary; his resolve had returned.

He noticed she was wearing a pair of short boots. She said Marguerite bought them for her in the village.

Transportation arrived in the form of a Toyota pickup truck without hubcaps and fenders, the paint chipped and faded, like a toy truck left in a sandbox over a summer of sun and rain. The drivers introduced themselves as the chief's sons, Adoum and Zigla. One was short, the other tall. Vincent saw no resemblance between them.

Zigla, the tall one, did the talking. He said they would drive them to a place where they could buy a pirogue, a papyrus canoe, and they could go by river as far as Sibiti.

Vincent was taken by surprise. He had not thought about traveling by boat; the rivers were polluted and dangerous, and the currents erratic.

"What river? And who is going to sell us a boat?"

Zigla answered, "We will take you to someone who knows where you can buy a boat."

Vincent turned to Angeline, "Why not take us by truck to Loubomo?"

"Too many checkpoints," Zigla said. "The river is the best way to get through the forest. But you cannot go further than Loubomo; there are waterfalls and the river flows into the Congo."

"Loubomo is half the distance to Pointe-Noire," Angeline said.

"Then walk?" Vincent asked.

Adoum answered this time, "There are dirt roads between Loubomo and Pointe-Noire."

"How many days walking?" Vincent asked.

"Maybe three," Adoum answered. "The roads are very bad." He looked over at Zigla who nodded in agreement.

Vincent turned to Angeline, "Do you agree with what they're saying?"

She gazed steadily back at him and with her eyes he was certain she said yes.

"Have French troops arrived in the area yet?"

"The French soldiers are gone," Adoum answered.

"How could that be?"

"They helped the *colons*, then they left."

"When?"

"Two days ago."

"For fuck's sake, it's not possible," Vincent said, excitedly. He had planned to travel along a route most likely to result in their running into French troops. He was counting on them being in the country. It did not make sense.

A pair of bats the size of crows flew over the patched roof of the hut. At the sound of their wings beating in the air everyone looked up into the dark sky.

Marguerite came out of the hut balancing the knapsack on her head. A machete dangled from her right hand and she clutched a rolled up blanket inside her left arm. When she gave the knapsack to Vincent, he noticed it was much heavier than when he had first inspected it. She had added jars of palm wine and water.

Marguerite and Angeline embraced. As Angeline walked to the truck, Marguerite made the sign of the cross. It was an image that remained in Vincent's mind that this purveyor of magic should also believe in Jesus Christ.

Adoum drove. Angeline and Vincent sat in the open back of the truck. There was no road, only a dirt track and the rough ride. They covered their mouths and noses with a blanket to keep from choking on the dust. The sudden flash of the truck's headlight exposed worthless possessions scattered and smashed, trails of tin cans and litter, and for a time they both felt like they were gagging on the strong odor of ash and dead fire, cinders, then nothing, the smell of burnt grass, the austere silhouette of a few banyan trees still standing across the desolation.

Vincent put his arm around her to prevent her from hitting her head on the sides of the truck as it bounced across the dirt.

"I can't recognize anything," she said quietly.

He gazed gravely at her without seeing her face. Separated from her by the black night, what answer could he give except to agree? "We are lost," he would have said if he had answered. But he did not answer.

He thought about what Adoum and Zigla had told them, that the French had left two days before. Could that account for why the night was free of guns and explosives? He looked over the side of the truck. There were lights up ahead and not long after they were passing an encampment of shacks, as many as a hundred, he thought, closely spaced, made out of corrugated strips of metal and iron, cardboard, mud, any scrap that could be used for a wall or a roof.

"Why, when there's so much empty space, are the houses always built so close to one another?" he asked, though it was more of an expression of bemusement than a question.

"They are afraid to be alone at night. It's too dark, too crowded by spirits. When everyone is close like this, it feels safer," she said. "This way they can ward off the night together until the oil in their lamps runs out."

Children began running after the truck as it struggled to fit through the narrow alleyway separating the rows of shacks. "*Cadeau, cadeau,*" they shouted. A few tried to climb onto the back of the truck.

Adoum stopped and jumped out of the driver's seat chasing the children away with his hands. They scattered like birds, then crowded back again, hanging on to the sides of the truck. "*Cadeau, cadeau,*" a boy pulled himself up over the side.

"*Pas de cadeau, pas ce soir,*" Vincent said. The boy remained squatting across from him with outstretched arms as other children climbed in the back of the truck.

Angeline broke out a handful of sugar cubes and gave them out. There was a show of excitement, and the children went off to enjoy the sugar.

A man accompanied Adoum to the truck and got in the passenger's seat in the front.

"Zigla can drive this time," Adoum said as he jumped in the back of the truck with Angeline and Vincent.

Vincent slapped at a mosquito on his arm. Blood, hopefully his own, he thought, spurted onto his hand along with the crushed insect.

Adoum said, "They are attracted by the heat from the engine. They smash against the windshield of the truck, sometimes so many, you can't see the road."

"What road?" Vincent looked over at Adoum and grinned. Adoum grinned back. In only a few minutes, once they were underway, they would be plunged back into darkness, strangers again, but for now Vincent felt he could afford to be friendly.

"Who is he?" Vincent asked Adoum, gesturing toward the man who had gotten in the front seat.

"His name is Marcel. He can get you a boat," Adoum answered.

"That doesn't answer who he is," Vincent said. To himself he was thinking too many people had seen them driving through the shantytown.

"He is powerful here. He has connections in the government," Adoum said.

"How is he powerful?" Vincent asked.

"Enough to get you a boat," Adoum raised his eyebrows and shrugged.

Vincent was not satisfied with the answer, but he knew he would get nothing more.

The truck stopped abruptly in a place that appeared barren; even the bush which was everywhere was not there. Adoum and Vincent climbed out the back of the truck.

"You have to walk from here," Adoum said. "Close to the river the ground is too soft; the wheels get stuck. My brother will wait with the truck." Adoum paused and shifted his eyes across the blank night. "We will need money for petrol for the way home. There is a petrol station."

There was no petrol station; Vincent knew it was a lie. It was suddenly pitch dark. Zigla had turned off the headlights. A moment later someone lit a lantern.

Angeline wrapped the blanket across her shoulders as if she were cold. The air was damp and torrid, and if it had turned cooler Vincent had not noticed; he was sweating.

"Wait behind the truck in case they try to rob us," he told her.

She seemed reluctant.

"There are three of them against two of us, and they know you're carrying money. They have to have at least one rifle stashed in the front seat," he said, betraying his frustration in his tone.

"Marguerite arranged this and they will not cross her," she said.

He wanted to shout, but he kept his voice low so only she could hear. "They are not afraid of Marguerite. Adoum has already asked for more money for petrol. You said Marguerite paid them. If they were afraid of her, they'd be afraid to ask for more. They'd fucking drive us to Pointe-Noire if they were afraid of her."

She did not answer, gazing back at him with her still eyes that only made him more confused.

"Say something in response. Say you hate me. For Christ's sake, I don't care as long as it's something."

"There is no choice but to trust them."

"No," he said, "maybe no choice but to pay them: we would be out of our minds to trust them."

When Vincent walked back to the other side of the truck, Marcel and Zigla were standing with Adoum smoking, the long trails of cigarette smoke hovered in front of their faces.

"I am a businessman," Marcel said, as if to reassure Vincent. He was a big man, with an open and audacious smile and a strong handshake. "I am told you are taking Madame Angeline to Pointe-Noire. You are right. Here it is no longer safe for whites. You especially will be recognized at once as a French soldier and an enemy. Against the whites it is a war of revenge. It is something different between ourselves, but I do not need to talk about that now. I am told you need a boat."

Marcel's breath smelled of cheap booze, though he was not drunk; he was surprisingly smooth, surprisingly undrunk, Vincent thought.

"You're a businessman," Vincent repeated. "What's your business?"

As he was addressing him, his eye fixed on the frayed edges of Marcel's white dress shirt that hung outside his pants. He wondered how old he was. Thirties maybe? Here it was hard to tell. A thirty-year-old could look fifty in the tropics. Too much sun.

"Simply, I deal in supply and demand," Marcel answered. "I know someone who will sell you a boat."

"What kind?" Vincent asked.

"A pirogue, a wooden boat. There are no motorboats. You'll have to row."

Vincent felt uneasy and suspicious. Here where everything was scarce, how was there an extra boat?

"What will he use when he sells his boat to us?" he asked.

"He has two boats. One belonged to his brother who drowned recently in a fishing accident. The money will go to his widow."

"You are sure he will sell to whites?" Vincent asked.

"I will tell him to sell. I will tell him the woman has the protection of the *féticheuse* and he will sell; he will be afraid of the *féticheuse* and he will sell."

Vincent kicked at the dirt with his boot. It was getting harder to conceal his frustration. There was always a reason for things that had something to do with fear or magic, things that one couldn't possibly contradict with logic or common sense. But these reasons were given inconsistently and as a convenience. He was supposed to believe this man would be afraid to defy the *féticheuse*. If the *féticheuse* were so powerful, why wouldn't Adoum and Zigla drive them to Pointe-Noire? Her so-called powers could buy them a boat, but not a car: it was insane.

"What do you want?" Vincent asked.

"Fifteen hundred French francs in advance. When it's time to buy the boat, the boatman will set his price."

"Have French troops been this far into the interior?"

"There is an airfield outside Zanaga. Do you see a single plane? The evacuations are finished. There is a cease-fire to give the French time to get out. Soon you will hear guns again. The fighting will resume."

There was no chance of being rescued now.

"I will talk to her," Vincent said.

He went to the back of the truck where Angeline waited.

"He wants fifteen hundred French francs," he said. "That doesn't pay for the boat."

Her face was as still as the bush at night. Yet now he was

sure inside she screamed and cried. Her still face was a lie the way the stillness of the bush at night was a lie.

She counted out the bills and gave them to him.

She must have seen him hesitate.

"What is it?" she asked.

He shook his head. The best way to Pointe-Noire had to be by truck, no matter what anyone said about the checkpoints. He felt the Beretta beneath his shirt, and he knew what he had to do. He thought for a second how to go about it—grab Marcel and take him hostage—he was the powerful one—kill the other two if he had to. Marcel would accompany them to Pointe-Noire, saying whatever was necessary at the checkpoints along the way.

He walked back around the truck to Marcel. A look of fear crossed Marcel's face; he knew. Yet he made no move, so Vincent felt sure he was not carrying a gun. Fortunately, Adoum and Zigla seemed distracted and unaware of what was about to happen as they leaned against the front of the truck, smoking.

Vincent took a breath, and was about to press his gun into Marcel's side when he heard her voice a few steps behind him.

"You can trust us," she said to Marcel as she approached.

The opportunity for stealing the truck had passed.

Marcel's face seemed to relax as he held out his hand waiting for Vincent to give him the money.

"Because of the *féticheuse*, I will come with you as far as the river," he said, addressing himself to Angeline.

Vincent observed a poignancy to his voice that was not there before.

Zigla stayed behind with the truck. Marcel led the way under the feeble guidance of the lantern along a semblance of a dirt path. The brush was about calf-high. Vincent kept Angeline close to him, walking in the rear, because no matter what she said, he did not trust Marcel or Adoum or any of them.

He could tell they were very close to the river. The air was so damp his skin felt wet as if it were raining and the mosquitoes were biting like crazy.

It was another hundred meters before they came upon a meager hut, its roof a mix of reed-thatch, planks and bits and pieces of corrugated iron. The ground surrounding the hut had been raked free of grass, and the smell of the damp red dirt was in the air.

A small bare-chested man wearing shorts made out of rags was standing in front of a burning fire, stoking it with precise motions. His hair was cropped against his head as if it had been recently shaved, and his front teeth were missing, which made him look like both a child and an old man at once. Nearby on a wooden block were cooked pieces of monkey meat; the flayed skin, washed clean of blood, was laid out in the dirt to dry.

Marcel approached the boatman. Vincent could not recognize what they were saying.

"What are they speaking?" he asked Angeline.

"*Lingala,*" she replied, "Marcel is threatening him. The cash for the boat will go to Marcel. In turn he'll give the man supplies he needs or bribe the local tax collectors for him."

"Why sell to us? We're white."

"He believes the boat is inhabited by evil spirits who caused his brother's accident. He knows no African will buy it. He thinks the evil spirits will follow us and leave his brother to rest in peace."

Her explanation left him feeling strangely at ease. At least it made sense out of what was going on.

He looked inside the half-open door of the hut. Children slept side by side on a straw mat. A woman naked from the waist up, sitting perfectly still like a scared rabbit, stared back at him.

"He wants two thousand French francs," Marcel said.

Vincent walked over to the boatman who was still stoking the fire, not oblivious to their presence, but unaffected by it. In the fire's light Vincent could see the ulcers on the man's hands and feet.

"Tell him instead of cash, we give him antibiotic for his sores."

The boatman's bloodshot eyes reflected confusion at why everyone was looking at him suddenly.

"They're tropical sores. You get them from walking through the bush," Marcel said. "If a few sores make you sick, you don't need a boat, because you will never make it to Pointe-Noire. You need a boat. You pay for the boat; what happens to the money is not your concern after that."

"The man has syphilis. Look at the corpuscle on the inside of his thigh."

"Two thousand if you want the boat," Marcel said.

"You will get your money," Angeline said coldly to Marcel.

"I am sorry," she said softly, turning to Vincent. "Even if Marcel were to get the penicillin, the dose would never be enough to cure him; it does not exist here in sufficient quantities." She was quiet for a moment. "The suffering is unto death," she said.

Unto death, the words repeated in his head.

"You stopped me from taking the truck."

"I was afraid, yes, because by truck between here and Pointe-Noire I am certain we would be killed."

His eyes remained on her face.

"You act like you don't believe me," she said.

He suddenly wanted to touch her again, and he put his hand to her cheek, waiting for her to pull back or to push him away, but she did not, only her still eyes staring back at him.

It was something he was taught in the army, remain still in the face of the enemy: it is a show of strength and the enemy will look for your weakness.

They made their way through the bushes to the riverbank. A narrow plank-built boat, gray, high sided and squared off at the stern, was resting against the trunk of a tree.

Vincent took the lantern and inspected the inside of the boat for leaks, touching the planks to feel whether the wood was rotten. It seemed all right, and he gave a nod to Angeline who handed Marcel the bills.

"Loubomo," Vincent said, pointing to the right bank.

The boatman nodded.

"Beware of the crocodiles. They are vicious and always hungry," Adoum warned as he gave the boat a shove.

When Vincent looked up, the three men had vanished.

CHAPTER TWELVE

Just above the water the air was cooler. The surface was calm. Yet he could feel the pull of the current beneath the surface. He rowed in silence, never really sure of how much time had passed or what distance they had covered. The shore was black despite the moon. Soon the sound of the oar breaking the surface became just another of the sounds of the night. He was concentrating on rowing and he lost track of her too, keeping his eyes lowered as if looking up at her might break his rhythm.

"You're exerting yourself too much," she said, holding out the jar of water for him to drink.

Without realizing it, he smiled.

"We have to make distance at night," he said.

"Drink and rest a moment. There's no harm. You'll see, in a little while the night will close in on us and we won't be able to do anything until the morning when the mist clears."

He had been afraid of that himself. He took the bottle and drank, then gave it back to her.

"Drink more," she said. "You're doing all the work."

"We both need our strength," he said, refusing.

They could smell the banks where the river narrowed. She lit the lantern and the boughs of the trees shook with bats. Afterward everything was still again, the high tops of the trees that hung like a canopy, the jungle that grew in between the trunks and the flat surface of the water, like the night itself, an immovable wall of darkness.

He kept rowing, more uncertain than ever of the time, though he guessed another hour passed that way. The lantern was useless in the pitch black night, and he feared it was too dangerous to continue. The rivers through the jungle were wild. The current could change abruptly. He threw the anchor, made of rocks tied together in a piece of net, only half convinced as it sank that it would suffice.

The lantern cast a stark white light across the inside of the boat. She was sleeping. He leaned over and swiped the mosquito from her cheek.

The temperature had dropped and it was so damp the air was wet. When he opened the blanket to cover her it was full of water roaches. If she had been awake, he would have asked her, maybe she would know the words to describe—insects, plants, trees, this miasma of heat and green, crawling, suffocating, maybe then when things had names it would seem more real. He leaned over and killed another mosquito, on her shoulder this time, thinking when he touched her arm that it was cold and there was nothing to cover her with.

He lay beside her, placing his arm beneath her head to protect her from the splintered and damp bottom. She stirred at first as if about to open her eyes, but she did not awaken. The warmth of their bodies drove the mosquitoes into frenzy. Yet neither the mosquitoes nor the dampness could keep him from sleeping. He felt the boat rocking from side to side. The heavy mist stretched from river to sky, like the vapors of a dream. He closed his eyes, unable any longer to tell the difference between reality and sleep.

Then it had been silent; only the flapping of the river against the sides of the boat, the hollow refrain of the crickets or the songs of the night birds, not sweet, but not harsh either.

It was different in the morning. He was learning. From night to daylight, here no lasting peace was possible; a few hours respite was all he could hope for. He was awakened by the anguished sound of women wailing. Surely, I am in hell, he thought.

"It is a funeral," Angeline said. "When they cry like that, it's for a child."

Her pale green eyes looked paler, clouded with white, and she herself seemed like an apparition across from him. The sound began to intensify, rising like a song. It was as if the suffering were in the air, in the trees when the air touched them and evoked a breeze. He had heard it called the "heart of darkness." Here darkness has no heart; it is merely the solace from the light, and the truth of the light was that unison cry of misery like puss oozing from an open wound.

"They will cry that way all day, until dusk, sometimes into the night," she said.

"How do we know the rebels weren't here?" The sound unnerved him and left him with the uneasy feeling of being vulnerable to attack.

"Here it's easy to lose everything. It doesn't take a war," she said.

She seemed sad rather than shocked. That is the difference between us, he thought. She has acquiesced, like adjusting to the heat or the humidity, and I will not allow myself to acquiesce no matter how long I am here.

The wailing grew more distant as he rowed. It was monkeys screeching or the raucous cry of birds flying in and out of the trees. The sun was a bright yellow ball of fire burning a hole through the white sky. It was between eight and nine in the morning, the hour when the sun burned through. The monotonous green brush stood in place of the fog. Long islands of lily pads, the white flowers nearly closed against the heat, covered over the brown water, and, along the banks, scattered thin trees rose up like sticks with crowns of half-starved branches where small birds with faded brown plumes perched.

The current was gaining strength. He tried to look ahead to prepare himself for what might be coming, but it was getting harder to see with the glare of the sun against the water. At night it had been too dark, now in the daylight there was too much light.

"You could go blind in this light," he said, looking over at Angeline who seemed to be growing weaker as the heat wore on. Her lips were parched and white. He reached out to her with the water jar. Her hand was covering her eyes as she drank. Her skin had turned very red. His own skin ached. She sipped some water and handed the jar back to him; it was hot like the temperature.

"We will have to find some place for the night down river as far as we can go," he said.

A silent acknowledgement passed between them that the night would be hard. They had no tent and the *moustiquaire* was not adequate protection against insects, bats and snakebites.

"Sibiti is not far; there is a hotel," she said.

Brazzaville was vivid in his mind, stories of whites dragged from their hotels during the night to be beaten and left for dead in the streets.

"We're safer in the bush for now," he said.

She looked up, as if she were waiting to meet his gaze. "The night is terrible here in other ways too," she said. "There were times I couldn't bear to be alone, and I would drive the four hours to Brazzaville to the Hotel de Ville. You have to fall in love here the same way you have to drink, because otherwise the boredom becomes too much. It was never passion. It's not possible in this climate. It's only the heat we remember."

The beautiful women in the bars in Djibouti City, willing to give themselves for the commission they received on the drinks the soldiers bought them—how many nights had he spent like that? Does she know, he thought, or is she asking me to tell her? It's been the same for me, pleasure for a night, maybe two, and, yes, I could walk away, always, and I did.

He saw her watching the shore expectantly. He wondered if she knew something he did not. He could feel the current pulling beneath them, and the boat picking up speed. The carcass of a dead goat swept passed them and he was able to judge how fast it had become. The river was about to grow wild.

It was no more than fifty yards across, but he had to struggle against the current to get to land before the river swept them along too, like the old shoes and dead birds or the broken tree branches. It was late afternoon; how late he was not sure because of the clouds covering the sky.

The water was shallow near the bank, and they walked to shore.

"There were no crocodiles. Adoum was wrong," he said.

She tied her skirt into a knot above her knees so it would not get caught in the underbrush as they walked. With her skirt that way and her hair pushed up off her neck, she looked like an African woman despite her light skin and soft hair, he thought.

Pointe-Noire was south and to the west. According to the compass, they could follow along the banks of the river, using the river as a guide for a while longer. He picked up a long stick and sharpened the end with the machete to look for snakes as they walked. The reeds cut at their ankles like razors, and the bush grew hydra-like around them even as he cut and hacked at it with the machete.

They came across a band of three feathers tied with a piece of string to the fork in the branch of a tree, bright colors, red and green and blue, parrot feathers. He swiped with the machete and cut it down.

"Don't," she said, trying to stop him, but too late. "You shouldn't have cut it down; it was left there for a reason."

He gazed directly back at her; there was hostility in his voice and in his eyes. "More voodoo. Not for anything real," he said.

"You're wrong. It could have been meant as a warning."

"Of what, a ghost—a spirit, a witch dancing in the trees? I don't believe it. It's ignorance, ignorance, all of it; I won't let it in my head."

He was losing his temper and he stopped himself, lowering his eyes and looking away from her. On the ground the feathers were already covered with red ants.

CHAPTER THIRTEEN

Sunlight fell between the trees in long columns of light. Angeline felt the urge to reach out and hold it in her hand. She had a sense of time passing, as if she could feel the ground shifting beneath her. The dream she had had in the pirogue started to come back to her. Patrick was in the dream. He had been away and she was happy to see him. It was morning and she was getting ready to inspect the orchards. From the bedroom window she saw the sun glistening in the tops of the trees. There were the familiar sounds of Patrick's footsteps in the hall, the clatter of breakfast dishes and the workers' voices carrying from the orchard. She must have been awake by then because she already knew it was a dream and there was the foul smell of the river in her nostrils; but she held on a few moments longer before she opened her eyes and saw Vincent lying next to her on the damp, rough wood and she let the dream go.

She took the machete and reached up into the trees for a vine. Cutting it open, she let the clear liquid spill over her hand.

"If it doesn't burn or sting, you can drink it," she said. She cut open a second vine and held it to her mouth.

"The trick is not to let the vine touch your lips."

Vincent cut a vine and drank the way she did, holding it above his mouth. Then later as they were walking, he sliced at the vines that blocked the path with the machete. Suddenly there was a spray of blood as if the tree were alive. There had been a snake hanging from the tree; he had mistaken it for a vine.

At five o'clock the mosquitoes descended, an onslaught of thousands. They pulled down their sleeves and buttoned their shirts to the collar.

"This must have cost a fortune," Vincent said, pulling out the mosquito repellant from the knapsack. They sprayed it generously over their faces and legs.

"Have you noticed how night falls more quickly in the forest?" she said.

It was already dark around them, though they could see the sky still light above the trees. Vincent continued to check the ground beneath the leaf litter for snake holes.

"We can stay here," he said.

He covered over the ground with palm leaves so it would be soft to sleep on. Then he lay down the plastic tarp and draped the *moustiquaire* across two bamboo sticks.

"Probably better to save the water for morning," he said, reaching into the knapsack. There was a jar of palm wine. He filled a tin cup and drank to quench his thirst.

"Awful stuff, palm wine, like a hangover without getting drunk."

He sat down on the stump of a small tree. The fire was burning by then as she stirred a polenta made with manioc and salt over the fire.

A bright red ant crawled on his leg. He picked it up, showing it to her. "In training camp they teach us which insects to eat to survive in the jungle. This for example, I could eat this red ant; the carapace contains protein."

"You won't have to eat it tonight." She pulled out a small tin of paper-thin cookies. "Patrick must have brought them back for Marguerite and she gave them to us."

They were butter cookies. They ate a little of the manioc, the salt made it palatable, then the butter cookies to take away the bitter taste of manioc and palm wine.

The mosquitoes were unbearable despite Marguerite's spray. He kept his pants tucked in his boots and his sleeves pulled down to the wrists, but he wondered about Angeline who was wearing a skirt.

Through the clearing in the trees there were no stars to be seen. She lit candles like the ones they had used on her veranda, the short wicks burning inside small tin canisters. They ate slowly and drank two cups of palm wine each, despite the unrelenting onslaught of moths and the streams of tiny flies on their hands and faces.

"You seem to be thinking about something," she said, and her voice broke him from his thoughts.

"I was thinking the night is very dark."

"It will get chilly too," she said. "That's why Marguerite gave us a blanket."

"The *féticheuse* thought of everything." There was a hint of sarcasm in his voice.

"Marguerite is a very thoughtful person," Angeline answered. "But let's not talk about Marguerite." Then changing the subject, "Where are you from?" she asked.

"Marseilles," he said. "My mother was from there."

"Does she still live there?"

"She died of cancer when I was eight."

"And your father?"

"I didn't have a father—not one I knew anyway. After my mother died, my aunt sent me to military school. She thought since my father was a sailor the military was in my blood," he shrugged. "There was one life, the one with my mother, and it ended when I was eight, and a different life started, one without any relation to anything before."

He looked straight at her as a smile emerged through his closed lips: "*Legio Patria Nostra*, the Legion is our Fatherland."

It was true; the military was the only life he knew.

Without warning, it began to rain violently, a heavy tropical rain like a wall of water. Thunder and flashes of colored lightning, pale ruby and pink. Like nothing I've ever seen before, he thought, as he watched in awe. He left the water jar out for the rain to fill. The rain was drenching, and they opened their mouths to drink the rain as it fell. The storm lasted a few minutes, followed by the empty sound of thunder.

Everything was still again, torpid as during the day; the rain seemed to have fed the humidity rather than cooled the air. The ground was too wet to sleep, and they had only the lantern for light. They sat without talking. He was trying to come up with a plan for the morning. How could he find his way when everything seemed without direction? Tonight there was thunder instead of explosives. The war seemed to have been lost somewhere, left behind in a landscape that had swallowed it whole, the way the orange sky swallowed the gigantic sun at dusk. They had not seen a person since the send-off by Marcel, Adoum and the boatman at the river. There had been the women crying, but how could he be sure it was not an animal mocking them in a human voice, or one of those spirits of the dead that everyone here feared, a fragment of a human soul lost forever in the forest? Surely anything was possible in such desolation, even the magic he dismissed as the work of charlatans.

He took off his shirt, and by the light of the lantern looked over his arms and legs for mosquito bites. There were scratches from the reeds. Moving one of the candles closer so he could see, he washed the scratches and the bites with alcohol.

"They're prone to infection; it's important to wash them well."

She pulled off her boots. He was struck by how well the snakebite had healed. He took a fresh piece of cotton and soaked it with alcohol.

"Hold out your legs," he said.

She pushed her skirt up to her thigh. Her skin was warm and smooth and it made him desire her again.

"It burns, I'm sorry," he said.

"We've both been apologizing to one another all day." She was smiling as she said it.

"It feels like there should be someone to blame for what's happened. We're just taking turns," he said.

They both agreed it would be best to sleep so they could start at first light. The makeshift tent, that was for her. He was used to sleeping out in the open; in the Legion they never used tents, though he would have wanted a *moustiquaire* for himself. He cleared a spot beside the trunk of the tree and put down the knapsack to lean on. Then he hung the lantern on the branch above him so he would be able to see in case he had to shoot.

When he finished he found her standing a few feet away.

She seemed to be hesitating. Her eyes glistened like two pools of water and the rest of her face was unnaturally pale in the light of the lantern. She was staring at him, staring boldly at his eyes as if she were looking through him.

"I don't understand the way you look at me," he said quietly. It was an honest thing to say.

Her eyes lowered and she did not answer. After a moment she said good night.

CHAPTER FOURTEEN

Through the blanket she could smell the earth, still damp from the rain and smelling like moss and clay. She looked over at Vincent. Through the haze of the lantern she watched him as he slept as she had on that first night in her house, when the fever had depleted him, and she remembered how she had felt then; it was as if the fever had ravaged her too and afterwards she was spent.

She ran her finger in the dirt, which was moist from the rain. Patrick had a mistress in Brussels. They never spoke of it. In a way it changed nothing because she had never felt for him in a way that excluded other love affairs. But maybe he loved the woman in Brussels. She had never thought about it before in this light. If he did love her, then she was happy for him.

The night seemed to close in around her. Strange, menacing sounds ruptured the stillness; they grew in volume and number as she listened, the unison cry of some bird or insect, each outburst followed by a silence that was all the more profound. The impenetrable darkness loomed everywhere she turned, and she felt defenseless like a child too frightened of the dark to sleep. And yet exhaustion and lassitude were lulling her into sleep against her will.

Suddenly in this half-sleep, she heard the branches shake as if someone were walking through them. Silence followed. The night the rebels had burned her house she had heard that sound. Panic possessed her sleepy body and made it tremble. She forced herself to open her eyes. Through the gap in the leaves she could make out the face of the man she had killed, standing there, black as night, but there was no mistaking his face, staring straight at her, neither angry nor sad, a face that had no expression. She tried covering her eyes with her hands and burying her face, but she could not make the image go away. She heard the branches crack and a new wave of fear gripped her. Jumping to her feet, she let out a terrified scream.

Her cry woke Vincent, who pointed the Beretta into the eerie stillness of the night. Seeing nothing, he quickly went to her and wrapped his arms around her shaking body.

"He is here," she tried to say, but the words remained trapped inside her. She felt his arms around her and she heard his heart beating, and the leaves seemed to close out the darkness and the face went away.

"Tell me," he said gently, stroking her hair to calm her.

"I saw his face through the leaves, watching me."

"Whose face?"

"The man I shot." Her voice trembled as she spoke. She would not look at him, or lift her face, which was buried in his chest.

"Everything was silent and I heard something moving through the leaves and then he was there, staring at me, watching me."

"You saw a big animal; it could have been a chimp or an ape, and it frightened the other animals," he said, gently lifting her chin so she would look at him.

She shook her head. Tears shimmered across her cheek. "He has found me and now there is no hiding from him; he will not let me go."

He held her very close to him, so close he took her hand and pressed it against his neck. His desire for her had become like the heat; he felt it in every look, in the scent of her skin, the urge to feel her hair, to taste her lips.

He drew her closer to him. His thigh touched hers and a sigh of pleasure escaped from her lips. She desired him, and when she tried to pull back, he would not let her.

"Why did you turn me away? Answer that first."

But she no longer had an answer, not one she believed.

She let her gaze meet his and she felt his breath on her cheek. He drew her mouth towards his and began to kiss her, holding her so tight against him as if he might devour her in an embrace, her body against his, all of her warm with desire, and he looking back at her with brooding eyes.

"We can stop here and go no further," she said in a voice scarcely more than a whisper.

He shook his head. "Tell me I don't have to hold back any longer—"

With her eyes she gave away the answer she could not bring to her lips.

He pulled her to the ground, and there he made love to her, suddenly, violently, their bodies drenched in sweat. He was on top of her and through the darkness he could feel her watching him, and he held her tighter, and as he embraced her whole body she felt like a wave swallowed by another wave. Her breath quickened beneath him and she closed her eyes.

The door had opened and the night had come in. They

had let it in. She felt him inside of her and she loved him and wanted him, and there was nothing left for fear. *The woman who loves him will cry long and hard in the night*—then let me cry, she thought. Something happened in that moment; everything that before had seemed hard now seemed easy.

The heat lingered on their bodies and left them exhausted, but that too felt good. He lifted her shirt and kissed her round breasts, full and youthful like her lips.

She spoke to him softly as she ran her hand across his shoulder and let her cheek rest against his chest. "I knew your body before tonight. I could feel your heart racing with fever; I rubbed your back and thighs with cool water. When the fever broke, I watched you as you slept."

He smiled, not at her in particular, at the night, at the idea of where they were and how they had gotten there.

She said, "When you smile you have a dimple, and your eyes stop brooding. I don't have to worry about you."

It was the change in his eyes, the way there was no longer any white beneath the pupil and she did not have to think of Marguerite's warning.

He let out a little laugh. "Is that what the *féticheuse* told you, that you have to worry about me? You don't have to worry about me."

"Will you smile all the time for me? As much as possible, anyway?"

He removed the hair from her face and traced the shape of her eyes with his finger.

"When I opened my eyes in the room in your house and saw you, I thought you were an angel. I came to Africa expecting to find oppression and suffering. I found you. Nothing is as I expected."

She placed a kiss on his chest, just over his heart.

"Now we're finished with all of our confessions," she said.

"No, there is one more. You are safe with me. Rest now. There is tomorrow."

The lingering heat had begun to dissipate and it was cooler. She was half-sleeping with her head resting against his chest. He lay awake listening to her breathing against the sounds of the African night, and her body felt warm and her skin was flush with sweat and lovemaking. The moon was up, a three-quarter moon, visible in the spaces between the trees. There was a direction now. The stars seemed to blur into long streaks of silver. He cradled her head in his arm and drew her gently against him.

"Before you I never knew love to be warm. Love was always cold and I could not warm it and I stopped loving."

"And now?"

He drew her closer and placed a kiss on her forehead.

"Now I know the difference between love and death," he said.

CHAPTER FIFTEEN

She woke up happy. He realized he had never seen her happy before.

The sun was not quite up. It was premature to call it morning, though the sky had lightened and the mosquitoes had abated.

He made a fire and she made coffee in the little steel coffee pot, good strong coffee. They drank it without sugar, boiling hot in the tin cups, and ate the last of the butter cookies.

"Did you have any dreams?" she asked.

He shook his head; he had been too exhausted for dreams.

"And you?"

She thought of the face she had seen gazing boldly at her through the trees. It seemed like a dream, though she knew it was not.

"I dreamt of you." She reached over to kiss him, and after kissing they both wanted more, but they agreed they would have to conserve their strength.

They packed up quickly. They traveled away from the river, out of the forest toward the savanna. Walking less than an hour they could see clearing, a grass plateau with acacia trees scattered across. In the distance there were large green hills and beyond that the tops of mountains.

A truck approached. The raucous engine became louder as the truck sped closer.

Vincent pushed her down in the knee-high grass. "Lie flat," he said. He felt his heart beating fast and the thin, steady rush of adrenaline through his body. They were wrong, he thought, Adoum, Marcel—what do they know? We've still got men here. They're coming to get us. With each rapidly passing moment he was surer of it.

He kept his hand on her back to keep her down as he peered above the grass just at the point when the truck came into view. He could see from the grille that it was an old Berliot. There was a gunner in the passenger seat, his *Kalashnikov* hanging out the window, and the torpid air had the smell of burning tobacco. Three men with guns and rounds of ammunition slung over their shoulders, wearing tee shirts and sunglasses, sat in the open back of the truck. His hopes were crushed.

There was no time for the adrenaline to stop. The man in the front seat fired, pulling the trigger with one hand. The truck kept going without slowing down. Vincent noticed Angeline fingering the *nkisi*, pressing the nail through the wooden case, and he gestured with his eyes for her to be still; the slightest movement could give up their location. A second shot was fired, again at nothing, before the truck drove off into the hills and was lost from view.

Angeline wondered if death were no more than that moment of dread stretched out over a lifetime of waiting, which, when the time came, would pass like the morning mist beneath the sun and be nothing. Then in her mind she saw the face peering through the branches, white as a phantom, the face of death waiting to even the score between them.

She folded her hand around Vincent's, and she felt him through her whole body. Before last night she desired him, but now she loved him and it made everything different.

She wondered if he had seen the look of fear cross her eyes. "Somehow the face I saw last night seems more real because they are here," she said.

He touched her brow with his finger. "Forget about what you saw last night," he said. "It was nothing. What's beyond the hills?"

"More forest. Maybe a *zone interdite*—you know, a game reserve."

"We're better off in the hills in case the first truck was a lookout and they're moving camp."

She could focus again, as if those few minutes of feeling his hand in hers had given her new courage.

"You think they're organized that way?" she said. "Your mistake is you still believe in order. Here randomness is the only order. They're a death crew, and they have one mission—kill as they go." Her voice quivered, though she kept it low.

"In my world there is an order," he said.

"Your world took off on a plane without caring about what happened to everyone they left behind. Your soldier's world is dead too; it's the same for you as for me. Nothing left."

He lifted his eyes to meet hers. "We have each other," he said.

When he said it she knew it was more than either one of them had ever had.

There was too much sun; it was that time of day, the hours of blinding glare and staggering heat. He wiped the sweat from his brow and with it the flies that had gathered there, attracted by the moisture.

The truck had disappeared. The hills emerged like an enormous oasis overflowing with beautiful shrubs. In the distance the light seemed shaded in a mist of lush green. He had that feeling again, that everything was safe. He knew by now it was a mirage, the hallucination of the desert traveler. Each time it would be interrupted, abruptly, violently, like a gunshot fired into the stillness.

As they mounted the hill, the silence was replaced by a rumbling mixture of noises. The hill was steep and he took her hand, but the further up they got, the louder the noise became. He ran on ahead of her to look. From the top of the hill he could see a procession going on below in the gap between the hills, bright colors, yellow and orange, standing out against the breathless landscape of grass and bushes. It took a moment before it registered: this unending parade of women and children was an exodus, strangely unhurried and beautiful to watch, walking with their possessions on their heads and their babies strapped to their backs.

After a few minutes, Angeline caught up to him.

"Why are they walking north?" he asked. Pointe-Noire was west.

"They are fleeing into the bush," she said.

The truck appeared again, as if out of nowhere. The front seat passenger was firing his gun into the air as the truck drove forward. The orderly procession dispersed into chaos. Women dropped to the ground, pulling crying children down with them. The truck stopped at the front of the procession, blocking the dirt path. All five men got out, their *Kalashnikovs* pointed into the crowd. One by one they made the women empty the sacks they carried on their heads.

One of the women became hysterical and resisted when they tried to take her sack. They beat her with the blunt end of the rifle until she fell to the ground, and they hacked her with a machete.

After they had beaten her, she lay motionless in the dirt, a scarlet pool of blood growing beneath her. A small boy threw himself on top of her and began to cry loudly, "*Maman, Maman, Maman...*" Then one of the gunmen fired. The boy stopped crying. His body became still. The gunman had shot the boy in the head and killed him.

Angeline let out a cry, and Vincent grabbed her and covered her mouth as he held her face to the ground.

"Quiet, if you don't want to die too," he whispered against her ear. He could feel her body rocking with sobs and he kept his hand over her mouth.

"What matters is staying alive. When they approach you, say nothing. Do not resist; they become more violent."

Minutes passed. He kept his hand over her mouth. The truck drove away in a cloud of dust, and the crowd of women and children moved on.

A flock of birds flew overhead across the red sky.

"There must be water in that direction," he said, though he knew it would have to wait until morning. It was almost dusk.

The smell of eucalyptus seemed heavier at night. When he lay down the ground smelled sweet. He rested on his side using the sack as a pillow as he waited for Angeline to come out of the bushes. He did not light the lantern for fear of who else might be camping in the hills. It was still too early for the moon to give any light. He called out to her in a low voice and she came running to him.

She kissed him and he could feel her heart beating fast in her chest.

He took her hands in his and they were cold. He rubbed them to warm them.

"My hands are often cold, even in the heat. Here they believe cold hands are a sign that your blood is cold."

"Your hands are already warm; I barely had to rub them," he said.

He held her tighter, with his hands inside her shirt feeling her warm skin, and he pulled her closer to him. She wrapped her legs around his. He took a deep breath of the cold air and felt the long warmth of her naked body beneath the skirt.

"I want you to love me hard. Leave nothing back, so I can forget today and think only of you," she said softly.

Her face was cold from the night air, but her lips were warm and he reached inside of her where it was warmer still. He slid his pants from his waist and held her closer, and he felt his flesh against hers, and everything was warm and damp. Then he was inside of her, and her legs tightened around him, and he could taste the sweet jasmine taste on her skin. She kissed his neck, his mouth. He repeated her name over and over, *Angeline, Angeline*…her sweet breath on his face, he went deeper inside of her.

It should have been slow. It should have lasted. He wanted to make it last. He could feel the cold against the sweat on his back, and it was over as he lay with her against him in the afterwarmth. He had this feeling there was no time for love to come slowly between them. He had only a few days to love her. In Pointe-Noire it would be finished.

He felt her hand, felt the thin gold wedding band on her finger.

"If it bothers you, I'll take it off," she said.

He shook his head. "No," he said. Compared to what they had witnessed today it seemed trivial.

"I did not make you forget," he said.

Her hand locked inside his.

"For a little while I forgot. When I felt you inside of me, there was more that was good than bad to living. Will you hold me?" she asked softly.

The cold was outside and he could feel her warm against him as he put his arms around her. She touched his chin.

"Your beard is rough," she said.

"Tomorrow I'll shave. There will be water at the bottom."

She kissed him lightly on the shoulder, and he held her face in his hand. The moon was nearly full. The selenium light caressed her face and she seemed more beautiful than ever. He was about to tell her he loved her when she put her hand to his lips.

"The evil spirits are listening. Never let them know what you love because they will destroy it. They are worse than those men today."

He pushed back the heavy frame of hair from her face and kissed her gently on the lips. There was no loneliness left inside of him. She had filled him, and he lay on his side with his head toward her, feeling her lips on his throat and her hair against his chin as he listened to the night noises. He ran his hand through her hair, feeling it soft and rising through his fingers, and it came to him that he had been living his life up until then believing in nothing, loving nothing, always waiting for someone to give the next order to fill the void he did not even feel because it had been there for so long. It could have gone on and on and he would not have known or cared, except that she had filled him and he did know and he did care.

At dawn he got up to relieve himself in the bushes. When he came back she was still asleep; beneath the white veil of mosquito netting she looked like a bride wrapped in white, he thought. From a few feet back he watched her in the early morning light. He was making a picture in his mind, something he could take with him—for later, when this was finished.

Angeline, I do love you. Though to appease her he did not say it aloud.

After an hour he woke her and brought her a cup of hot tea. He stroked her hair.

"We've got to keep moving," he said.

He saw her fumbling in the half-light for something on the ground as she lifted the blanket.

"I thought I had lost it," she said, holding out her open palm.

"What is it?"

He recognized the object; she had been fingering it as the gunmen passed.

"It's called a *nkisi*. Marguerite made it for me. I push it down when I am afraid."

It must have fallen off while they were making love. She tied the knot around the broken string and put it back around her neck.

He wondered if she was afraid now. He thought he knew the answer; he felt it inside of himself, the terrible fear that comes with love.

The sky was becoming light and birds were cawing loudly from the trees. It was still cold as night and he wrapped the blanket around her shoulders for warmth.

CHAPTER SIXTEEN

By the time they reached the river on the other side of the hills the sun was burning in the sky and it was hot and airless. There was a stench from far away. As they got closer, they found the river was polluted by corpses tied and thrown into the water like bundles of sticks.

At the girls' school in Brazzaville in the evenings an old woman walked along the edge of the forest with wide, open eyes. The girls were frightened of her. They never knew where she came from or how she got there. Sometimes they heard her voice without seeing her. The girls believed she was a zombie—a dead person who appears to be alive or a living person who appears dead; there is no difference, Angeline thought. That is why the gunmen did not see us in the grass. We have crossed the line where it no longer matters whether we are alive or dead.

She could smell the dying grass and dry leaves. She was unaware that she had stopped walking and was standing beneath the sun as if she were asleep.

"Drink," Vincent whispered, holding the water to her lips. It was warm like the sun, not cold like her blood, she thought. Vincent gazed at her, the face she loved, the lips she hungered to kiss. It came back to her so quickly; she was alive, but too weak to say it aloud.

"There's no point in resting where there's no shade," he said.

They kept walking west. They were getting closer to Loubomo, the midpoint in their journey. The day was spent cutting through the mountain passes, moving swiftly and silently.

"Here it is harsh, but Loubomo is very green, you will see," she said.

They drank the dregs of palm wine, bitter and warm, and they ate the last of the manioc. Tiny flies swarmed their faces and hands.

The sun had disappeared and everything was bathed in diminishing red light. Though the heat had not abated, the approaching dusk promised relief from the sun.

"Africans believe the jungles are full of zombies. Do you know what a zombie is? They cry in the wind in one voice, wandering through the jungle, no different than the spirits of the dead who wander. As I was walking I had the feeling that I was no longer among the living."

"You were dehydrated. It happens quickly; the mind starts slipping."

Whereas he felt the green trees closing in on him, she felt herself disappearing, becoming so lost, as if she no longer existed.

"We are not zombies," he said. "We just need water."

A few feet away a bush lit up in hundreds of tiny lights like a Christmas tree. Then the cloud of iridescent light lifted into the night sky.

"Fireflies," she said.

The fireflies flickered across the night from bush to bush. The air had turned blue with nightfall, and it was damp, and in the dampness there was a chill. Vincent made a bed out of palm leaves. How many nights like this can we survive? Without water she might have died today. We are both becoming weaker, he thought.

He looked at her crouched across from him, her face drawn by exhaustion into some hollow resemblance of a pretty girl. He remembered how full her body had seemed when he first noticed her that morning in the kitchen of her house. She was strong-willed and courageous. Yet there was something broken and vulnerable about her. Behind her steady gaze she quivered. He had to love her before he saw it. She was bent over the open knapsack, looking for something. When she stood up, her body was like a long shadow against the night air, which had turned the color of blue ink. And in his mind he saw her walking with all of her possessions on her head, picking up and leaving at a moment's notice, on the move like the women in the hills with nowhere to go, their misery following them like the mosquitoes and flies.

She lay next to him and buried her face in his shoulder as she clutched his hand. He felt the moisture of her breath warm against his skin, and he put his arm around her and drew her closer and he felt a heaviness overcome him as sudden as the dusk.

He must have fallen into a deep sleep because he did not hear her get up. He heard a cracking sound, as if something were breaking, and he woke with a start and felt for his gun. She was sitting beside a small fire she had made from brush. The sound he heard had been a branch breaking apart in the flame.

He came closer and warmed himself near the fire.

"I was cold," she said. She sat with her arms close to her chest.

The blue was draining from the light and they could see the moon fading through the openings in the trees. They put the fire out with dirt and went on. It was not far before they came to a narrow river. There were flowers growing along the banks, dark brutish red, open wide, greedy for more sun. A flock of blackbirds flew down to drink. Angeline took off her blouse and washed. Her nipples were round and pink beneath the sun, soft at first, then hard when he put his lips to them.

He made a fire and boiled the water to make it safe for drinking. She lay down to rest, and he left her and went to the water's edge to shave. The black birds took off at his approach. He looked at the razor, the blade reflecting the sun and almost disappearing in the brash light. Why would Marguerite have thought to buy him a razor? It was the inconsistency that unbalanced him, how one action did not follow from another.

He splashed water on his arms and face. Then he sat watch with his hand resting against the handle of the Beretta as he looked around him. It was a beautiful place—wild, untouched. Yet he knew what he saw was not real—it's what it hides that is real, he knew that now. She was resting with her eyes closed, and when she opened her eyes and saw him she smiled. He thought she too is part of the secret of the place, something he did not understand, but wanted.

Dense forest awaited them on the other side of the mountains, ready to swallow them one more time. After about an hour's walking they could see a village clearing in the trees. The tops of the huts were covered by large birds, and from where they were they only saw the birds, like a dark cloud hung too close to the ground. As they got closer they could recognize the sour smell of blood; the odor grew in their noses and mouths until they could taste it in the air.

The huts were all the same, small and rectangular with mud walls and grass and tin roofs. Low trees that grew out instead of up were scattered along the outskirts, and the vultures perched across the top branches were making a horrible frenzied noise.

Vincent remembered an African soldier telling him one night over a warm beer, "The villages are where our grandparents live. Everyone else has left for the city."

Trails of black smoke wafted into the sky from fires left to extinguish on their own. They heard a cat crying in the emptiness. Then it stopped and there was only the greedy cry of the birds. He fired a shot and the birds dispersed.

"Wait here," he told Angeline. Her eyes were large and frightened. He breathed deeply, as if he could take in enough air to avoid having to breathe inside one of those huts.

"Vincent," she called back to him. She bent down and tore off a strip of her skirt. "Wear it to cover your mouth and nose," she said.

Inside the first hut he found the bodies of two women and a small boy lying together in a pool of black blood, their throats had been slit and their flesh torn by repeated blows with a machete. Flies stuck to the open wounds where the blood had dried. They were already stiff; they had been dead for hours.

He went from hut to hut. In each one it was the same, women, old and young, and children, so many children. Only in one hut was an elderly man. His throat had been slit and his testicles cut off.

It was becoming harder for him to go through it, to see

children stiff on the floor and smell the rotting flesh and the too sweet odor of blood as thick as cotton. He thought he was going to scream or collapse on the dirt floor; he could feel the scream rising in his throat, so he began to move more quickly, to go in and out without thinking or stopping.

It had happened at night while they were asleep. Some just had their throats slit; they never woke up. Others were hacked by machetes. These were the ones who had struggled, especially the children, who must have become hysterical and tried to escape; their bodies were cut up the worst.

He stopped counting the bodies. He could not bring himself to look at the faces covered with flies.

He went in to each hut just enough to satisfy himself no one was alive. He saw the little bodies huddled on the floor in a pool of blood so close he could not have told them apart, an arm, a leg all mixed up, in death they were one. And in a corner a woman whose back was turned to the wall, the children's mother, no doubt. He did not fault her for turning her back. How could she bear to watch? But he was thinking now and he could not think because if he started to think he would lose his mind, so he stopped seeing, and when he stopped seeing the thoughts stopped coming.

He was going out when he heard a cry, feeble and high-pitched, not a human sound, but the sound of something alive all the same. The sound in that space of corpses froze him in place. He heard it again coming from the corner of the room where the woman lay dead. It was the same cry they had heard from outside, a cat he had thought then, though now he was less sure. He took a cloth from the wall and wrapped it around his hand, because the risk of disease with all this blood was too great. He heard the cry again before turning the woman over. His throat went stiff and his breath seemed to get caught in his chest as if he were reacting before he knew or believed. An infant lay huddled beneath her breast—a baby boy, when Vincent lifted the woman, the infant squinted his eyes as if even the shadowy daylight inside the hut were too much for him. She had been hiding him. This explained why her back was to the other children. Her flesh was no longer warm or soft and the infant lay beneath the stiff heaviness of it, like a stone gradually crushing him.

Vincent lifted him in his arms and walked out in the drenching sunlight to Angeline. A look of horror had overtaken his face. He feared for what he would have to tell her, so he said nothing.

She took the infant and cradled him gently, turning him toward her to shield his eyes from the light, but letting the heat of the sun warm his tiny body. He seemed weak from crying. She went beneath the shade of a tree and sprinkled a mixture of water and sugar from the tips of her fingers into his mouth. The infant opened his eyes and began to move his lips, stretching for more. She held him close and fed him little spoonfuls of the sugar water.

Vincent's legs felt weak as if he could not stand and there was a sound he kept hearing. He did not recognize it at first, then he knew; the vultures had returned. He pressed his face against the mud wall. The odor of mud was in his nostrils. He could hear the words in the voice of his commanding officer in his head, speaking with the conviction of God and country, the way men who have stood knee deep in shit and blood are allowed to speak. *We are not here to fight. This is an evacuation mission. What happens in this war is not our concern.* Words were good for some things. Words were good for lying. He pounded at the wall of the hut until the mud began to crumble in his hands and the smell of mud replaced the smell of blood everywhere in the torpid air. He thought he was going to vomit, but the feeling passed and he wept instead.

He remembered Angeline and the infant and he got up and went to her. She was sitting in what little shade there was beneath one of those thin trees, holding the infant in her arms. She had torn off another piece of her skirt and swaddled him in it.

"He was thirsty," she said. "He is hungry too." She did not look up as she spoke but kept her eyes fixed on the baby. There was a sweetness to her face.

"He is healthy. His mother's breasts must have been full of milk."

Vincent knelt on one knee. Her eyes met his, but he averted his gaze as if he were afraid she might be able to see what he had seen, that it might still be there, reflected in his eyes.

What she did see was the sickly yellow pallor of his face, the tears that clung to his eyelashes, and she thought of Marguerite and of the unhappiness she had predicted for him.

He lowered his head. "All dead." He did not say more for fear his voice would break.

When he looked up at the sky again it had turned golden. It was noon.

"He will need milk," she said softly, calling his attention back to the infant and away from his thoughts.

Vincent knew they would no longer be able to seek out the deserted routes. From now on they would have to go where there were women because the baby would need to nurse. Shielding his eyes with his hand, he looked across the terrain. The trees were too thin, the bush too still, the sky too immense above the thick, suffocating canopy of green. At last I know what you hide, he thought.

When he looked back at Angeline, her eyes were on the infant against her breast. As the terrain had become immense and unmanageable for him, it had become so small for her. She held the infant close to muffle the sound of his small, painful cry unto a heaven all too accustomed to suffering to care whether he lived or died.

"We will find where those women and children were going," he said.

They headed into the bush. He knew they should have gone west to Pointe-Noire, but they went north and headed into the bush.

CHAPTER SEVENTEEN

They could hear the noise before they saw anything, the unbelievable racket of thousands of women and children cramped together in the jungle, setting up camp in the dirt and trying to recreate some semblance of the life they had known, but without men or food or nearby water or latrines. The air had the stench of an open sewer. There were chickens and goats, pots and pans and small cooking fires by the hundreds where handfuls of maize and unripe bananas were being cooked into a stew that would keep everyone alive another day.

When they entered the camp people stopped what they were doing to look. The quiet began to spread. People stared, not knowing what to make of them, the French soldier and the white woman with the black woman's baby, Angeline with her hair, wild and knotted and falling down her back, her tattered skirt, the mud from the hut on Vincent's face like dark paint, the baby crying—how had they wandered through the jungle to the camp? What did they want?

"The baby needs milk," Vincent shouted.

There was no answer, only the look from eyes, black and piercing, staring back in silence everywhere.

"They think we are possessed by evil spirits," Angeline said in a low voice. "They are afraid."

Vincent shouted out into the crowd. "The baby will die. He needs to nurse."

"The white woman has no milk for a black baby," a woman shouted back from a few feet away.

"What about the white cockroach, she doesn't want to give her milk to a black baby?"

Angeline did not answer. The baby continued to cry as if stirred by her trembling body.

"White women have white cockroach milk," another woman shouted.

Then another, "White poison in your white breast."

"White cockroach, white poison."

It was one voice, one face, repeated over and over, everywhere Vincent looked. Stretching out like the bush as far as he could see, those eyes staring back at them with a look at once hostile and frightened, open, exhausted, eyes haunted by fear and animated by hate.

"You are wrong—it's hate, not fear," Vincent said in a low voice to Angeline. Then he turned his steady gaze back on to the crowd.

"His mother and family were murdered by the same people you have come here to hide from," he shouted.

But they did not seem to believe him or care.

"White cockroaches killed the baby's mother," a woman shouted. She wore a large yellow and green scarf like the kind Marguerite wore wound high upon her head.

A boy in the crowd threw a stone hitting Vincent in the shoulder. Angeline turned her back to shield the infant, expecting more stones to be thrown.

Vincent pointed his gun into the crowd.

"You can hate us and the baby will die. Is that what you want? Another innocent life."

There was silence, more stares, more waiting. They were too far gone in their hatred to care about innocence. The baby was crying, a high-pitched constant cry. Vincent knew if they ran now, they would be pursued and in the madness of the moment killed. They had to stand their ground so as not to appear weak.

Angeline nervously fingered the *nkisi* around her neck.

Close by a young girl, her hair cropped to her head, bare-chested, her breasts just starting to mature like two small plums, began to shriek and point at Angeline, who knew at once the girl was frightened of the nkisi. The girl believed she was cursing her.

As the girl's shrieks began to draw attention, Angeline shouted into the crowd.

"I am protected by the *féticheuse*. She will know if I am harmed, and she will harm those who harm me."

Whereas the gun had only quieted them, the threat of the feticheuse appeared to frighten them. Vincent looked at their faces, the endless sea of eyes turning from hostility to fear, from something hard and fixed to trembling like the air in the light; a rusty nail hanging from a string had more power over their hearts than the dying infant.

The crowd backed away. Angeline took a few steps forward, approaching a short woman with a baby in a sling on her back.

"The rebels murdered his mother and brothers and sisters, but he was unharmed," she said, meeting the woman's gaze head on. She had large brown eyes with a tinge of blue in the whites.

Two young children clung to her skirt, crying in a shrill, fearful whimper. She took the baby from Angeline's arms, and exposing her long full breasts, began to nurse him.

A crowd began to form around the woman. The little ones at her skirt stopped crying, squatting in the dirt to watch.

After a few minutes the baby stopped sucking and the woman handed him back to Angeline.

"Enough for now," she said. "He becomes sick if he drinks too much at first," the woman said. "He is special. The devils were afraid to kill him. *Fils de Dieu.*"

"*Fils de Dieu*, God's son," Angeline repeated. What the woman said struck a chord in her. "*Fils de Dieu*," she whispered, casting her eyes over the sleeping baby, as if it were a prayer. "He belongs to God."

She looked over at Vincent who was looking into the crowd; he seemed tired, preoccupied. A woman presented her with a sling to carry the baby. Another woman brought a basket. Throughout the afternoon there were gifts of bananas, maize and tea. Angeline knew it was because they believed it would bring them God's blessings to have given a gift to the baby who frightened the devils.

"They believe he is special to God," she said to Vincent. "*Fils de Dieu*, the woman who nursed him said. Now he will be known by that name."

"Anything that attracts attention to us is bad," he answered.

An old man, whose name was Jean-Bosco, approached them and began to talk to Vincent. He said he was sixty, old for the Congo.

"The French forgot you were here," he said. "They came last week to get out the *colons*. You are forgotten like us."

Forgotten, the word echoed in Vincent's head.

"Where are the rebels now?" he asked, turning his attention again to Jean-Bosco.

"Scattered through the countryside. They had to hide when the French came."

Jean-Bosco cleared his throat and spat a thick wad of yellow mucus. He was drinking a warm beer, banana beer; it was everywhere in the Congo, warm, too sweet, but easy to get drunk on. The alcohol or maybe just the dust from the camp had made his eyes bloodshot.

"I heard the rebels raped the white women. They rape all the women. They go in the houses at night and steal the girls. That is why you need a strong door in the Congo. When they rape the white women, the French take it personally. They come with guns and planes when they rape the white women."

He stopped talking and stared straight ahead before taking another sip of his beer.

"How many villages have come here to this camp?" Vincent asked.

"Ten, twenty, all the villages upcountry from Sibiti."

"And what about Sibiti itself?"

"Maybe the rebels are there, I don't know. The rebels go to the villages. They take the men and boys for soldiers, give them a choice, die right now, or fight for the rebels. So they fight for the rebels and they get guns and machetes and they ride in trucks showing off their guns."

"Why camp here?" Vincent asked, though he wondered if Jean-Bosco knew, whatever his answer, whether anyone here knew except that there were others here setting up camp when they arrived.

"If we are together the Americans will give us food and supplies."

Vincent shook his head. "The rebels are nearby. Less than

twenty-four hours ago they massacred a village not far from here."

"I don't know about that," Jean-Bosco answered. "Too much hashish. They get crazy. They have to prove themselves." He shook his head. "I don't know about that."

He cleared his throat again, this time without spitting. What Vincent had told him seemed to have affected him and he seemed less sure of things.

"The women don't want to be alone without the men. They think they are safe here." He shook his head again. "The rebels can come here just as easy."

"Why did you come here?"

"I am a plantation worker. The *colons* left; the plantations are burned to chalk so there is no work. I can't stay alone in the village. If I had been young I would have done like the others and joined the rebels. Now I am waiting for the government to help us. If we are together we are easier to find."

Cholera would surely get there before the government, Vincent thought. In the afternoons the stench became unbearable. People were using the spaces in between tents and the ground was wet with human waste.

Jean-Bosco tried to straighten his knees, which appeared stiff with arthritis.

"Is anyone still living in the villages west of here?" Vincent asked.

"There are always villages along the road. There is a convent a day's walk from here. Twice a year I go to the convent. The nuns give me pills for the pain in my knees, a whole bottle. Good for six months, then I go back."

Aspirin, no doubt, Vincent thought. He shaded his eyes

with his hands. There was no shade in the camp, tents made from rags, plastic, blankets, anything that could be hung over a long stick, meant only for sleeping, the rest of people's lives was conducted out in the open. Noise, too much of it, laughter, fighting, like a gigantic platform in a train station, the bodies pressed too close together.

The afternoon wore on and the heat thickened. Children crowded around them and stared with wide eyes. Sometimes they giggled inexplicably. The rest of the time, in repose, their faces were fearful and expectant, and just a little sleepy, a demi-sleep brought on by hunger and heat.

A tall girl offered Angeline a drink from a tin cup. Vincent grabbed the cup.

"You don't know if it's safe."

"I am thirsty," Angeline said.

"The line is five hours for water," Jean-Bosco said. "Beer is easier to get. That's why I drink beer and only go for water twice a week. But to get beer you need money."

The infant began to cry again. Angeline handed him to a young woman with almond-shaped eyes and a sweet face. He seemed to suck for a longer time now, a sign of strength.

Vincent had intended to leave him behind with one of the women from the camp. After seeing how burdened these women were, how vulnerable to disease and attack, it seemed unthinkable.

It was not safe for them to stay in the camp; not just the risk of disease, the death squads would show up, if not tomorrow, the next day or the day after that. When they did, there was no question they would kill them for being white in a black camp. They would have to or they would lose their power over people.

Angeline lay with her head on the knapsack, the infant resting on her chest. What would happen when they reached Pointe-Noire? She imagined the streets drenched in sunlight, the sea in the background, and Vincent, clean-shaven and dressed in his uniform, waiting to say good-bye.

She drifted into sleep, and then she had a dream. There was a dark hall with a narrow elevator, the kind they have in hotels because foreigners insist on elevators. The elevator ride seemed interminable, though she remembered it was only going to the second floor. The door was jammed and she had to bang on it to get out. Her room was across the hall. It had been light on the street, but it was dark when she opened the door to the room, and she looked for the light along the wall. The sheer white drapes were blowing into the room. She could hear a sound, like the moan of the sea and she went to the window. Vincent was waiting for her behind the curtain. There were tears in his eyes. "Why are you crying?" she asked. He did not answer her. And she began asking what it meant, and Marguerite said, "Hold him or you will not be able to bear it when he leaves."

It must have been somewhere between two and three, because the heat had not disappeared. The moon was bright. Vincent pressed the baby close to his chest to mute his cry.

"Hurry, we have to leave now," he whispered to Angeline who awakened at once with a gasp.

The dry grass cracked beneath their feet. He kept looking back over his shoulder to make sure they were not being followed, but there was no one, and the camp was no longer visible in the night. A sense of sadness seemed to hover above the darkness and the silence.

Africa was that way, he thought, a few steps in a particular direction, and the night would swallow everything behind you as if it never were.

They were far enough from the camp to wait until daybreak before going any further. The infant let out a cry when he handed him back to Angeline, as if the change of arms had disrupted his sleep.

"*Calme-toi, calme-toi, ma biche,*" she whispered.

CHAPTER EIGHTEEN

Before noon they came to a freshwater pool surrounded by rocks.

"I'll be back," Angeline said.

"Where are you going?"

"To the water."

The water reached above her waist. She held the baby to her chest and wet his tiny body with cool water poured from her cupped hand.

Vincent waited for her at the edge of the rocks. A flock of red parrots lit on the empty branches of the trees.

"Africans believe a baby has his mother's blood and his father's spirit," she said as she dried the baby and wrapped him in a blanket. She spread the tarp and left him to sleep in the shade.

The sun was brash at this hour. Vincent went for a swim. Angeline let her legs dangle in the water. A little laugh escaped from her lips. For that moment of flickering sunlight she seemed happy, insouciant.

"Come," she said, pulling at him to get out of the water. "There is a spot where the ground is soft."

He followed her to the top of the bank where the grass had pushed its way through the hard dirt. The bottom of her hair was wet and it clung to her back. As she undressed, he felt desire swelling inside of him, and he wanted to touch her, and yet he stopped himself, choosing to hold time still, enough to take her in with his eyes, the gentle curve of her shoulder into her sunburnt arms, her breasts crowned by pinkish nipples, erect and waiting to be devoured by kisses, the round curve of her hips and the bush of dark hair, the contrast of her body, dark from the sun, and the part of her that was hidden and pale where he desired to bury his lips. He drew her to him; it was all there in that embrace, desire for her, love, the need to feel her flesh burning against his.

"Angeline," he uttered her name, as if her name could give a face to the immense sky and the menacing desolation.

She threw back her head and let him kiss her breasts, her neck, and he felt the sun as if it might melt them and they would become one, holding her tighter and pulling her to the grass which she called soft but to him was coarse. He was thirsty for her, for the jasmine taste of her lips. Desire raged inside of him like fever, like the scorching African sun on his back. She opened her legs and he held her tight, feeling her thighs pressing against his as he entered her. He was dizzy from the heat, breathless, and his body, moments before cooled by the water, was covered in sweat.

Afterwards, he kissed her tenderly, resting his face against her neck, feeling her fingers in his hair.

"Shall I tell you my dream?" she asked. "The one I have when I am not quite awake, yet not asleep either. We arrive in Pointe-Noire and say good-bye. Then at night when I return to my room I find you there waiting for me."

"Were you happy to see me there?"

"More happy than there are words."

He traced the line between her eye and mouth with his finger, and she closed her eyes for an instant. She did not tell him the rest of the dream, the tears in his eyes when she saw him or what they might mean, only how happy she was that he had come back for her.

He was about to kiss her, to love her all over again. There was a noise from above, benign, yet startling, that caused him to pull from her with a start and look up. Children were watching from the tops of the rocks, laughing and squealing. Little girls covered their mouths with their hands and pointed at them with long thin arms like sticks. Somehow the idea that they had been watching made it all seem terrible and awful.

Vincent got up abruptly to get his clothes. There was a look of anger in his eyes when Angeline took his hand and held him, gazing steadily at him.

"It's the Garden of Eden, Vincent, and we've been caught naked."

"To hell with Africa," he said.

The children ran away. He could hear them squealing and giggling as they ran.

He leaned against a rock and covered his face with his hands. He had a sense of terror as if he had just awakened from a bad dream. By loving her, by giving her name to the unforgiving sky and the relentless day, he thought he could change the feeling of having no control. But it had only made it worse, mocking them for their love now too. What price would they pay? There would be a price, he was sure. There had to be a price for love in this place of misery and hate.

She took up a handful of dirt and held it in her open palm.

"It would mean nothing to me to lose you, like losing a drop of mud," she said. "You mean nothing to me. Tomorrow I could wake up and forget you."

Then she opened her hand and let the dirt spill out. He gazed back at her, confused, saying nothing. Hadn't she just minutes before told him she wanted him to stay with her in Pointe-Noire?

"The wind will carry my words to the evil spirits who are listening, and they will leave us alone," she said quietly, with a look in her eyes both knowing and vulnerable at the same time. "Your turn now, tell me I mean nothing to you: If we'd never met, it would not have mattered."

He pressed his hands to her face, letting his eyes meet hers. He did not say it.

CHAPTER NINETEEN

Through all of this the infant continued to sleep, even when Vincent lifted him in his arms.

"He is sleeping too much," she said. "He needs to nurse."

"There has to be a village nearby. Where did those children come from?"

The children had disappeared as if they too were a dream.

The sun was hotter than before against the dirt. Vincent saw a narrow clearing in the trees and brush up ahead. This is the track Jean-Bosco spoke of, not wide enough to fit a car through, but enough to walk along, he thought. He looked down at the baby whose eyes were shut and holding the tiny white lips open with his finger spit saliva into the baby's mouth.

You have never experienced anything like the sun in Africa. It doesn't stop. It burns right through you. Too much of that sun changes you for life.

He remembered sitting in the officers' club in N'Djamena

drinking whisky at four in the afternoon, listening to the men who had been there for years, taking it in along with the air conditioning and the sweet aftertaste of the alcohol on the leftover ice in his glass.

He felt the sun pulsing against his head, burning through him as if he had no skin. It left him feeling exposed. Like the children's laughter at the rocks ringing in his ears, he looked over at Angeline.

Whatever you do, don't sleep with the women here. Too much disease. You won't feel like it anyway, too hot.

Had anyone told him not to fall in love? Above all else not to be so foolish as to love anyone?

The infant's silence was now as awful as if he had been crying, a sound like the midday sun ringing in his ears.

Children were playing on the outskirts of a village along the hillside, the same children, no doubt, who had been watching them, Vincent thought. They stopped playing to stare, giggling, pointing—Vincent kept walking, looking straight ahead, and the children became silent as if frightened when they saw him.

A pigmy sat outside one of the huts smoking a handmade cigarette with his short legs stretched out in front of him in the dirt. Vincent walked past him and swung open the door. A woman, her close-cropped hair covered in a faded blue scarf, stared with fear as a baby lay sleeping on a mat and a little girl played with a straw doll. The little girl began to cry loudly.

"I will not hurt you," he said, taking the woman by the

arm. She tried to break away and he tightened his grasp and dragged her outside where Angeline waited with the baby.

Once the woman saw what was wanted of her she stopped resisting and took the baby. When the baby was finished sucking, the woman handed him back to Angeline.

"I will pay you for something I can use as a diaper," Angeline said.

The woman went into the hut and came out with two squares of cotton the size of handkerchiefs.

Angeline took off her wedding band and gave it to her. The woman slipped the ring on her thin middle finger. She seemed pleased. She said she never had a Western ring before, looking at it against the glare of the sun; the gold seemed to light up like a flame.

"The direction of the convent, which way?" Vincent asked. His voice sounded stiff from dust and heat and thirst.

"The convent is along the road," the woman said, pointing in the direction of the dirt path.

"How long will it take to get there?" he asked.

"By tonight, if you are fast and do not encounter the buffalo. The buffalo come out of the forest to graze. Then they disappear back into the forest and no one sees them. Beware. The forest buffalo is very dangerous. You see it in front of you and in back at the same time, and then it tramples you," the woman said. She was smiling to herself again, looking down at the ring.

"It is very small, very thin, not much gold. Good gold?"

"Yes," Angeline said. "It is good gold."

The woman nodded her head in seeming approval. Other women came for a look at her prize and she held her finger into the sun. The women laughed.

Vincent could feel the sweat dripping down his face. He squinted into the harsh sunlight.

"*La bas, la bas,*" over there, the woman said, pointing in the direction of the convent.

The children followed after them, free of concern, like children anywhere, he thought.

"They are playing," Angeline said. "You will see, they will follow up to a certain point, then they will turn back."

He could hear their voices, the sound of their legs brushing against the dry grass. Then it was silent, and he looked back and they were gone.

As the woman from the village had warned, forest buffalo were grazing up ahead. He had never seen a forest buffalo before; they were slightly smaller than caped buffalo, reddish rather than black. They stopped grazing and breathed through those enormous nostrils, low, guttural, antagonistic, audible even from a distance.

Angeline refused to go any further.

"They are the most dangerous animals in Africa, very stupid and very unpredictable. The slightest shift of light or sound might startle them and they will stampede us."

He held out the compass to show her. "Southwest—the convent is southwest of here. We have to go in that direction." His voice betrayed his frustration. Exhaustion was taking its toll.

He was convinced they could continue around the buffalo without much risk. She, however, was adamant. He knew he would not be able to reason with her. For a moment he looked at her as if he were trying to understand. Her eyes quivered like the air trembling in the afternoon heat, and her lips seemed to be straining for breath. He understood her less than that first night on her veranda when they had argued. Yet in spite of this, he knew the bond between them could not be broken. They headed off in the opposite direction, away from the herd, but away from the convent.

They went south as if they were going to Loubomo. The area through which they traveled was cultivated for small farms and commercial agriculture. They walked through a field that had been burnt to ash and the destroyed *colon* house alongside it. The frame was still standing in places, but the inside had been emptied and devoured like a carcass. Vincent took some ash in his hand. The ash was black and it smelled of smoke, and he was certain it could have been no more than a week.

"*Douce, Doucement, ma biche,*" he heard the sound of Angeline's voice, "Softly, my doe," against the impatient cry of the baby.

The thing you must understand about Africa is that the boundaries are purely artificial; it is the same people from the same tribes from one country to the next, and it is therefore very easy to move from one place to another, to infiltrate country after country. It is a continent of countrysides, not countries, of tribes rather than governments. And of course tyrants.

Yes, Sir, I understand.

He was a young soldier then.

Angeline placed her lips on his shoulder, and he closed his eyes. The threat of dusk was in the sky, the orange burnt-out light that signaled nightfall—when he knew her as he knew himself.

CHAPTER TWENTY

They reached the convent that morning. They saw the cross on the roof from the distance and when they got closer, the long, concrete buildings in the clearing.

"When things are made of concrete here, it is because they are meant to last," Angeline said.

The grass had been cleared into powdery dirt that sprayed in a small cloud of dust at their feet. A skinny little girl, barefoot and wearing a denim blue shift, was chasing chickens with a broom as they approached.

The baby had begun to cry, and the sound frightened the chickens because they began to run in circles and make a lot of noise. But the girl had lost interest in the chickens and was staring at him. Vincent noticed her eyes; they seemed out of place with the rest of her, as if they had been drawn onto her little body.

A white woman in her fifties, her smooth gray hair pulled back into a bun, and wearing a crucifix on a leather string around her neck, came out to greet them. They introduced themselves.

"I am Sister Catherine," she said, shading her eyes against the sun with her hand. She was not dressed in a habit.

"Lt. Chavanne and I have been on our way to Pointe-

Noire since seven or eight days ago. I am a coffee farmer from Lekoumou," Angeline said. "My farm was burned by the rebels."

Sister Catherine took in what Angeline was saying without changing expression. "Pointe-Noire has remained safe," she said. She glanced at the crying baby, "He is hungry."

Angeline nodded. "We found him in a village near Sibiti. He survived the massacre there."

Sister Catherine took the baby from Angeline. "He's only a few days old. You're in luck. A woman gave birth last week." Then she turned to Vincent. "Lt. Chavanne, the French soldiers were here over a week ago," she said.

Everything confirmed what he already knew; it was too late to hope for a rescue.

Another girl, this one a little older with a pretty face, came out of the house humming a song. She was wearing a white dress with tiny brown flowers, and a brightly colored scarf tied tight around her head. The dress was short in the waist, as if she had recently grown too tall for it, and her bony knees jutted out. She looked them over before fixing her gaze on Vincent and giggling. When he looked back at her, she quickly lowered her eyes.

"Phalie," Sister Catherine called. "These people are thirsty. Please take them into the house and offer them something to drink," Sister Catherine said before disappearing with the baby.

Through the window they could see two nuns bending over a vegetable garden. They were African, and unlike Sister Catherine, they were dressed in a dark blue habit.

It could have been fifty years ago, Vincent thought, there was no way of telling; time had stopped here.

Phalie, still humming to herself, was squeezing lemons into a jar. Vincent caught her staring at him, her eyes alive with a playful malice. But his mind was on Angeline who seemed weak, and he gave no attention to the girl's stares. He reached out his hand and placed it over Angeline's. When their eyes met, she had a vague look as if she were withdrawing inside herself.

"It's the heat," she said softly.

Vincent looked over at Sister Catherine who understood at once.

"There is a bed in the back room where you can lie down," she said.

The room had a painted white iron bed and a crucifix hanging next to the bed above a nightstand. The shutters were drawn to keep out the heat and the room was shrouded in gray half-light.

"It would be better if you drank a little more," Vincent said. He had brought the glass of lemonade with him. The weakness was as much from dehydration as from exhaustion, he thought.

When he pushed the hair back from her forehead, her eyes seemed larger, more dreamy, and her face looked older, the frown between her eyebrows deep as if cut by a knife.

She began fumbling with the buttons on her blouse and he took her hand and brought it to his lips before letting go and undoing the buttons for her. Her chest was glistening wet with sweat, and he noticed her ribs showing through her skin. How fragile her wrist seemed in his hand.

Holding her in his arms, he made her drink again.

"I'm so tired," she said, apologetically, and she rested her head on the pillow.

He lifted the hair from her neck. "Sleep, *chéri*," he said softly, kissing her.

When he turned to leave he found Phalie standing in the narrow foyer, staring boldly at him, defying him to meet his gaze—she had been watching the whole while. He heard her giggle loudly as he walked past.

Sister Catherine was in the kitchen. The little girl they had seen chasing the chickens was crying, her face buried in the nun's skirt. She looked up when she heard Vincent's footsteps, then she began to cry again, burying her face deeper into the nun's lap.

"Amelie is frightened of you because she believes you have come to take her back to the rebels," Sister Catherine said, gazing with sincere eyes that seemed to Vincent to have grown accustomed to suffering.

"Please tell her I have nothing to do with that," he said. "Tell her I will not hurt her."

Sister Catherine rocked the girl gently in her arms.

"He is a French soldier. He saved the baby from the rebels. He will protect us," she said quietly, holding the girl's head close to her chest as she spoke.

"I will go out," Vincent said, not wanting to upset the child further.

Sister Catherine stroked her forehead. "Amelie will be fine."

The little girl looked up from the nun's lap, studying Vincent with her old eyes for a moment. Then she got up and went outdoors to play.

"Amelie ran away from the rebels and came to us. On the day she arrived she told me they killed her sister—beat her to death with a machete—young boys, boys she knew from the village all her life. The rebels threatened to kill the boys if they did not do it. Amelie told me the story when she first arrived. Then she did not talk for a year. Now she will say *yes* and *no*, but little more. When I first examined her, I saw she had been raped, not once or twice, but daily. We've seen it before. Other girls. We tend to their bodies and make them healthy. But there is nothing we can do for their hearts."

Vincent looked through the door. He could see her playing with a doll in the dirt. She seemed to have forgotten that moments before she had been afraid.

"Is Madame Bousquet ill?" Sister Catherine asked.

"Just exhausted, I think." He rubbed his hand along the rough stubble of his beard. "We've been walking in the heat without decent food or drink." His eyes met the nun's. One of her eyelids hung lower than the other; it seemed heavier as if there were an extra fold of skin.

"She has no fever?" Sister Catherine asked.

"No." Vincent shook his head.

"Sometimes the fever hides; it's there but it does not show itself for another twenty-four hours. In the meantime you are weak with all the symptoms of a fever."

An internal fever—he'd heard of it before.

"She's sweating," he said.

"Sweating is always a good sign in the tropics."

You perspire. White people come here and they don't sweat; the climate too much for their white skin. Marguerite's choppy French resounded in his head.

Phalie was breaking eggs to cook lunch and there was the strong smell of coffee.

"After you have eaten I will give you a tour of the infirmary," Sister Catherine said.

Vincent nodded silently. Phalie turned from the stove to glare at him again, a playful, devious look, before turning back around and tossing her head to the side, giggling comically. He noticed that Sister Catherine paid no attention to her behavior.

"We have cows and chickens," Sister Catherine said. "We grow vegetables in the garden and we have banana trees, so there is always food here."

Phalie poured out two bowls of café au lait and brought them to the table with a plate of fried eggs. He drank a few sips of the coffee, feeling it hot in his chest as if he could breathe for the first time in days.

"Phalie, it is time for your reading lesson," Sister Catherine said.

Phalie wiped her hands on a towel. She was still staring at Vincent, waiting for him to look up at her, but he continued drinking the coffee with his eyes lowered. He was confident she did not have the attention span to keep at it for long, and after a minute or two she went out of the room singing to herself, the same melody as before, a melancholy song, though she did not seem to know or care if it were sad.

"Her mother named her Encephalie because she had sleeping sickness while she was carrying her. Everyone calls her Phalie. She came to us with her mother and two younger brothers who had AIDS. They died and Phalie lives with us now," Sister Catherine said, with no trace of sadness or pity. It was a fact of life, an irreversible condition of existence.

Vincent lifted his eyes to meet the nun's stoic gaze, but said nothing. Anywhere else it would have been unbearable; here it was part of life. Still he felt bad. It helped explain the girl's odd behavior.

"Have the rebels been here?"

"They came," Sister Catherine answered. "We refused to leave. Many of our patients are dying and are too ill to be moved. I am a medical doctor. Several of our sisters are trained nurses. We are needed in the area. The rebels took our supplies, penicillin, needles, syringes, alcohol—things they might need, things they could use themselves or sell. Someone had been shot in the shoulder and needed to have the bullet removed. The rebels left and the French soldiers came. They brought new supplies to replace the ones the rebels had stolen."

She stopped, appearing to be listening for something, a noise from outside. Whatever it was, she was satisfied it did not require her attention.

"The rebels have moved closer to the Angola border where they are supported by the government."

He devoured the eggs. There was bread made from wheat flour and butter, and he ate two pieces. Sister Catherine poured more coffee; it was no longer hot, but it tasted good, especially with the milk, which was sweet.

"A woman was brought here by her husband for treatment. The rebels had raped her while her husband was made to watch at gunpoint. He was badly beaten. They considered themselves lucky because he was not killed."

She said everything in that same soft voice, the same plateau of emotion without hills or crevices.

"The army does not come out this far; they are in Pointe-Noire. They only come to the villages to collect the taxes."

"Are you afraid of the war?"

"I am afraid of what the war will do. We are a hospital. I believe we will be safe from the fighting."

He studied her face for a moment. She knew as well as he that the rebels were not rational.

He put his fork down on the plate and pushed it slightly forward.

"The army should protect you," he said.

"They have not offered," she answered. "The French wanted to evacuate us, which would have meant leaving our African nuns and patients behind; it was not a tenable solution or one the Church would have agreed with."

What right does the Church have to object? He did not say it aloud, as if he knew what her answer would be: There is God to protect us.

She got up from her chair. She had none of the gestures women had, the way women touched their hair or straightened their blouse. She did none of those things.

"Let me show you the infirmary," she said.

He looked in on Angeline before going out. She was asleep, her face buried in the pillow, and her long hair like a slow-moving brown river across the white sheets.

On the way to the infirmary, Sister Catherine called his attention to a small building with a painted gold cross above the doorway gleaming in the sun.

"That is the chapel," she said. "The priest travels from Sibiti to say mass. Then he stays on to administer prayers to the sick and to give last rites. The distances are great here, and the resources few."

They entered the infirmary through a side-door. Long rows of white iron cots were placed close together. At the far end of the room a girl was on her knees washing the floor with a brush. The sheets were white, and the wood floor and walls were clean, the way nuns knew to make things clean, scrubbed and smelling of vinegar. He had watched his mother die in a room that smelled that way.

Sister Catherine put a stethoscope around her neck and began going from cot to cot, speaking softly.

"Over the past ten years there has been recurrence of cholera, sleeping sickness, tuberculosis. Many of our patients come here to die of AIDS, mostly women who need help in caring for their children."

She stopped to listen to the heart of an emaciated man who was lying motionless, though his eyes were open.

"One might think there is nothing to be done for the dying, but that is wrong. We keep them clean. We provide them with a bed above the floor, blankets when they are cold. We assure them we will see to their burial and not leave their bodies to be eaten, which is a great anxiety. We wash them before we bury them and place a cross at their grave."

Sister Catherine's feet made no sound as she walked across the dry wooden floor, another luxury, wood instead of dirt. Vincent looked down and noticed she was wearing sneakers.

In the children's ward Sister Catherine went to each of the sick children in turn and brushed the flies from their nostrils, kissing them gently on the forehead.

Vincent saw the infant nursing. The woman lay flat on her back, staring distractedly at the ceiling.

"In the refuge camp they called him *Fils de Dieu*. They said God protected him and sent the white cockroaches to save him."

He clenched his teeth as the round of images went through his memory, coming upon him suddenly, the bloody insides of the huts, the faces in the camp, eyes, hostile and filled with fear—

Sister Catherine took the infant in her arms and checked his eyes and listened to his tiny chest with her stethoscope.

"He is healthy," she said.

Vincent bit down on his lip. "Then he will live—join the rebel army same as any who by some miracle survive, be given a gun and a machete and taught to kill, to rape—the end of communism, the beginning of democracy, what difference does it make?"

"You must be tired," Sister Catherine said. "You should rest. We have our meal just after dusk when it is first dark, and we welcome you to join us."

Vincent remained for a moment watching Sister Catherine lift a little girl in her arms and cradle her as if she were a baby. "They need to be held," she said. "Sometimes it's all we can do for them."

Once outside, he shielded his eyes against the white sky. How monotonous the daylight was here, exposed and unfiltered like an overhead light. They sang a song in the Legion,

Dans le ciel brille l'étoile qui lui rappelle son enfance
Adieu mon pays jamais je ne t'oublierai

He had never been nostalgic for his youth; nostalgia, sentimentality, these were indulgences he did not allow himself. Yet for a moment he felt a longing to be in a place where the light slanted across the wall and peeked through the trees, or as a boy in Marseilles, the way sunlight and shadow chased each other along the sides of buildings, a place where light was pretense, not as here where the light was true and everything was revealed in it. He thought of Marseilles, of blue sea enveloped by mist and the white ripple of the surf breaking against the shore; these too were the memories of his childhood, before sickrooms and unhappiness. He needed to be near the sea. On tour in Djibouti, during *sieste* he would go swimming in the Red Sea. It kept him sane. He had been too long inside this jungle.

He found himself in front of the chapel. There was no one there so he went inside. Within those dark walls, he felt a sense of calm, the room free of the oppressive green that was everywhere, quiet too, free of the taunting songs of birds and monkey cries.

He took a seat on the splintered bench. There was nothing on the walls, nothing to look at, only the crucifix above the altar. He stared straight ahead at the figure on the cross, carved from wood, the face a little longer, a little thinner, more crudely done than the portrayals he had grown up with in Europe, yet the symbol the same: one man's suffering meant to embrace all the suffering in this life.

It was a while, sitting in the shadows of the mud walls, before his mind gradually let go of the images that were haunting him. He was no longer sure that God owned the world. It was enough for him to be able to utter aloud the two words that came to his mind, "Help us."

When he got up his knees were sore and he felt the weight of fatigue throughout his body.

"Is there some place I can sleep?" he asked the first sister he saw.

She was African and she seemed shy in his presence.

Without lifting her eyes she took him to a narrow room in the back of the main house with a cot covered with a sheet that smelled of bleach.

He stripped to his underwear and sat down on the bed, holding his throbbing head in his hands. The girl, Phalie, was standing in the narrow hallway outside his room, a broom resting against her thigh, watching him, but he drew the mosquito netting over the bed and turned facing the wall, covering himself with the cool sheet and giving himself up to sleep without another thought to the girl or the baby or anything else he had seen in the past twenty-four hours that could break him up if he let it.

CHAPTER TWENTY-ONE

It was already dark when Angeline awakened. Outside she heard talking, soft, benign, women's voices at table.

She dressed and went out. The nuns were sitting outside for their evening meal, the black immoveable night surrounding them like a wall. There were flies hovering over the food which had the slightly too rich aroma of roasted peanuts. The Sisters were eating out of bowls rather than plates, with forks like Europeans. This was their meal for the day, their chance to socialize. Candles illumined the long wooden table. Sacre Soeur was the name of the order; Angeline had read it printed on a piece of paper on the nightstand in the room where she had slept.

When Sister Catherine saw Angeline she gestured for her to join them, making a place next to her.

"Witch casts her spell on you," Phalie said in a sing-song voice just above Angeline's ear as she put the plate and fork down in front of her. Then she smiled, a little smile full of malice, and, even in the dark, Angeline saw her eyes come alive with delight.

"Phalie, stop at once," Sister Catherine said, firmly, like a teacher reprimanding a pupil.

"Witch, witch, witch," Phalie muttered under her breath in

her sing-song voice, and she laughed aloud, a short, forced laugh.

"She dislikes me," Angeline said. "Have I offended her?"

"You've done nothing," Sister Catherine answered in a manner intended to end the subject.

Angeline's throat was so dry after sleeping it ached as she drank.

"I believe Lt. Chavanne is sleeping," Sister Catherine said. "He was exhausted. You both were."

A large bowl of *pate d'arachide*, mashed peanuts in spices, and *saka saka*, a stew based in manioc leaves, was being passed around the table. Angeline could smell the soap on Sister Catherine's hands as she passed the bowl of rice. Serene, Angeline thought, the word to describe her. Not so of the others. The African nuns, with almond-shaped eyes that make an ordinary face pretty, pushed up by high, jutting cheek bones, and full purple lips, pretty, but not serene. Too lively for that, even beneath their navy blue habits, a liveliness they could not contain, like the flame flickering above the candle in spite of the still night air.

Sister Catherine introduced her to the other nuns. There was Sister Marthe and Sister Agnes and Sister Rose, and they came here like Phalie and the other little girl who was chasing the chickens in the dirt, because somebody was sick or somebody died and Sister Catherine cared for them. They believed in their hearts what Sister Catherine taught them, that the sick and the poor and the unfortunate are Christ's chosen ones. Tonight beneath the flickering candlelight and the shadow of a hundred moths, they were smiling. Only the older ones who came from France, Sister Bernadette and Sister Berthe, were not smiling. They came here believing it was their job to nurse and to feed Christ's chosen ones, and in so doing to become one of them. Angeline remembered at the girls' school in Brazzaville they had prayed for shade; where everything was brightness or dark, the sun blazing, the girls prayed to God and to all the saints to protect the trees in the convent garden that they might give them shade. They had prayed for Christ's chosen ones too, but not nearly as hard as they had prayed for shade.

As they ate, an endless stream of large black ants made their way across the table, the nuns futilely brushing them away with their hands. Angeline caught Phalie glaring at her like a sulking child, hateful and with no ability to hide what she felt, before directing her attention back to Sister Catherine's serene face, and to her own thoughts which were of Vincent and the morning when they would leave the convent, and always when she thought of Vincent, of what would happen when they reached Pointe-Noire. She felt a heaviness overcome her and a sense of the meaninglessness of everything.

In the distance suddenly there was a loud rumble, the things on the table began to shake noticeably and they could feel the ground trembling. A few moments later they heard the cry of a forest elephant tearing across the night, a sound familiar to everyone at the table, yet terrible all the same. The candles shook and moths fluttered in the air like smoke. No one moved. From the sound, the elephant was close by. The other noises disappeared inside its cry; even the lowliest ant knew to obey that sound. Everyone at the table remained silent, listening, not knowing what the next few minutes held in store, whether the elephant would charge through the trees. Then the sound grew fainter; the elephant was going off in another direction.

"There is God who rules in heaven and the elephant who rules in Africa," Sister Catherine said, calmly, as if this were an ordinary occurrence.

The meal resumed, but its pleasant ease had been disrupted, and they hurried through the rest, gathering the bowls and clearing the table as fast as they could.

Afterwards Sister Catherine took Angeline to the infirmary. An oil lamp gave off a faint light in a corner of the room, made fainter still by the mosquitoes clinging to the sides like a shade. A child was sitting up in bed looking with wide eyes, as if waiting expectantly, though the child's expression never changed even as they approached, the eyes remained wide open, staring without seeing.

There were no cribs; the infant was asleep in a laundry basket on a table. Angeline bent over the basket. In the light of the lantern she watched the sleeping face, the pursed lips and the nostrils flared and quivering with warm breath. His little chest heaved a sigh as if he were dreaming. She rested her hand on the dried out edge of the basket and readjusted the little blanket that the nuns had swaddled him in. He seemed content, sleeping with his hands above his head.

"It's a sign of health when a baby sleeps this way," Sister Catherine said. She had finished her quick check of the other beds. They whispered so as not to wake the sleeping children.

"What will become of him?" Angeline asked, looking up from the baby.

"We will keep him here. We have powdered formula so we will not need to rely on someone to nurse him. I will try to find an African mother to take him. They are always willing to take in a child."

Angeline nodded. "I want to provide for him in some way," she said. Reaching into her pocket, she handed Sister Catherine ten thousand francs, most of what she had left, an enormous sum for the interior of Africa.

"You are very generous," Sister Catherine said, holding the francs in her closed palm as if to conceal the money from anyone who might be watching.

Angeline kept the remainder, a few thousand francs, she did not count it; but she knew she would need whatever was left to pay the bribes at check points as they got closer to Pointe-Noire.

"What are you going to name him?" Angeline asked. "Or will you leave it to the mother who takes him?"

"Is there a name you like for him?" Sister Catherine asked.

"My father's name was Paul," Angeline answered. She thought of her father for the first time since any of this began. He seemed mixed up with all the other memories, and she had been avoiding any thought of him or what he would have done in her situation. Somehow it seemed fitting to her, when it was all finished, her father's legacy would be an orphaned African boy bearing his name.

"Paul," Sister Catherine repeated, looking down at the sleeping infant, her voice so soft her lips hardly moved. "We will baptize him Sunday at mass."

She put her hand on Angeline's arm, and a second later her attention was diverted as if she had been called, though she was not. Something caused her to go over to the child sitting on the bed with wide, expectant eyes. Taking the child in her arms, she rocked him or her—Angeline couldn't tell—the child's head had been shaved bald and he or she was dressed in an old tee shirt. After a few minutes the child lay down and slept as if all along he had been waiting without knowing how to ask for that little bit of comfort.

"It's quiet now," Sister Catherine said. "When one child cries, they all cry. You will need your sleep if you are going to set out in the morning."

"And not you? Aren't you going to sleep?"

"I'm going to stay here a while longer. It is important for me to read the charts at least once a day."

Angeline surmised there was another reason. Sister Catherine was giving up her bed to her for the night; the room with the white bed and the nightstand where she had slept during the afternoon was Sister Catherine's.

She held the pencil poised between her two fingers, "Now I must read," she said. "The hours before midnight are the only quiet hours. The sick do not sleep through the night."

CHAPTER TWENTY-TWO

In the pitch dark Vincent thought it was Angeline until he heard the laugh which went through him like a shot, and felt the skin touching his, not smooth like Angeline's, thicker, more coarse. It was the girl, Phalie, sitting on his bed, pressing against him, her chest uncovered, her girlish breasts, tiny and firm, like two little cones. He could smell the sweet oil on her skin though it was too dark to make out her face.

She put her hand over his and tried to draw him to her naked breast but he resisted.

"Why have you come?" he asked sternly.

"You like my breasts? Feel for yourself. When you touch them you will know they are better than hers."

He remembered she had been watching as he undressed Angeline.

"You should not have come in here."

By then his eyes were becoming accustomed to the dark. He opened the shutter. There was enough moonlight to make her out sitting half nude on the bed.

He heard a bird chirping nearby, not a nightingale, not a song by any means, but a repetitive shrill sound, an insect sound, constant and annoying. He could have lit the candle near the bed, but he chose not to. The moonlight was bright enough to see her face, the sad full lips shaped into a frown, the thick eyebrows and her large glistening eyes. She tried to place her lips against his as she pressed her perfectly flat stomach flush against him with her little breasts, which would not have fit inside his hand if he had held them as she wanted. But he pushed her away, gently but firmly like a parent scolding a child, placing his hand around her wrist to restrain her.

"I will make you happy," she said in her sing-song voice.

That way of thinking, happy—sad, a child's way of thinking; she was a child.

"Take me with you away from here. You go to Pointe-Noire. I heard you tell Sister Catherine."

When he did not answer at once, she said, "You make my heart hurt if you say no. I will die if I stay here."

"Doesn't Sister Catherine treat you well? You are clean, well fed. What is it?"

"Things are possible in the city. Nothing is possible here. I stay here, I die like *Maman* and *mes frères*, I get thin and die in my bed like everyone who comes here."

How could he blame her for being afraid of what might happen here or expect her to understand that she was lucky because they put a roof over her head, fed her and taught her to read?

"I am not able to take you with me."

She started to sob, and he was worried she would wake up the house. To quiet her he rested his hand gently on her shoulder.

"If I were a white girl you would take me to Pointe-Noire like you take her when you leave here."

"That is not true. The city can be a terrible place for a child on her own. What will you do there?"

He knew perfectly well in the city she would become a prostitute.

"How old are you?"

"Eleven? Maybe twelve. *Maman* used to know. Since *Maman* is dead, there is no one to tell me my age."

He could see the white gleam across her eyes and the dark pupil like part of the night.

"I stay here and I die or I become a sister like Sister Catherine. Neither is good for me, to die or become a sister."

She tried again to force her mouth against his.

He could taste her saliva even as he pushed her away.

"You don't think I'm pretty?"

"I think you're very pretty."

"You will take me to Pointe-Noire?"

He shook his head in the dark, unsure whether she was even looking. This time he took her hand, small and childish inside his.

"It is not safe," he said.

She started to cry again, a very childish cry, and he put his finger over her lips to make her stop.

"You'll wake everyone."

Her small, childish hand clutching his, sweating against his palm—he held her hand until she pulled away. She seemed annoyed with him, already bored by his refusals.

"You take her with you. Safe for her? I know the answer same as you. Pretty white girl." The sing-song had returned to her voice, the malice and contempt that had been part of her stare all day. "A bird flies into my hair before *Maman* dies so I know witch cast her spell on me. Then *Maman* dies and I cry and cry. Last night I see witch cast her spell on your pretty white girl too."

She rolled her head back and forth and looked at him a last time as if she were mocking him. She left then.

He lay listening to her footsteps disappearing down the hall. He could hear the night noises through the open window. A cock crowed loudly, and afterwards other cocks began crowing. Someone was moaning in the infirmary. He listened, waiting for it to stop and after a while it did. He turned over and slept till morning when Angeline came to wake him. She brought coffee that smelled delicious.

"You slept through dinner," she said. She was smiling. She looked rested and clean and very young, the sleep reflected in her face, in her eyes, shining like water in the sunlight. Her hair was washed and her clothes were clean. She looks like a botanist he thought, here from France to do research for an article, as if she were waiting for her guide to arrive.

"I ate with the sisters. We ate outdoors despite the ants, *pate d'arachide* and *saka saka*. It was all very good. I saw the baby after dinner. He slept in the infirmary so he could nurse during the night. They have powdered formula that they can start to give him."

He finished the coffee in a few large gulps for he was thirsty, and she took the bowl from him and set it down on the floor.

"I spoke to Sister Catherine. The baby will remain here. African mothers are generous. There is the chance a family might take him."

He smiled. "It will work out for him," he said.

He looked out the shutter left open from last night. The branches hung limp from the dark green trees, and the sky was thick and white.

148

He reached over and wrapped his fingers around her forearm. "I can get to Pointe-Noire in a day. In two days I'll be back for you. Wait for me here."

She lowered her eyes. "What if something happens to you? What if they don't let you come back for me and I never see you again? I am going with you," she said.

He saw her expression, her eyes large and unyielding, so sure of herself and so strong. He knew it would have been futile to argue with her.

Phalie was in the kitchen. She glared at him before walking out of the room. In a sad way, he had almost forgotten about last night's scene. In the daylight she looked even younger, like a child already grown old inside her child's body.

Sister Catherine came into the kitchen on her way to the infirmary. She was carrying a tray with a large pitcher of mint water and a pot of tea.

"I know Phalie is restless here," she said. "I want her to stay a few more years until she is fifteen and I can get her a job in the hospital in Pointe-Noire."

Vincent said nothing. He wondered if she had heard the girl in his room. Nothing had happened. There was nothing to hide, still he felt awkward.

He stepped outside. Amelie played hopscotch in the dirt while a small boy leaning on a crutch watched.

It was better to start early, he thought; they could travel as far as fifteen kilometers by afternoon. The sky was white, but it hurt his eyes to look up. He washed quickly, feeling no more refreshed afterwards, as if the place could no longer be washed clean from his skin; it was part of him now. Whereas Angeline had seemed more sure of herself, to him everything seemed shrouded in uncertainty—Angeline standing in front of him with the baby in her arms (*They will name him Paul. Why Paul? It was my father's name*), the people in the infirmary dying slowly but inevitably, the two girls, Phalie and Amelie, and all they had endured (*If I stay here, I die like Maman and mes frères*), his mind was wandering, his thoughts breaking up against his will. No, he could not let it get to him; he had to keep going—for her sake now too.

"There is a dirt road from here to Pointe-Noire. We have a truck," Sister Catherine said. "I could drive you in a few hours' time, but there is not enough gasoline to take you. The refilling station has been shut down. The rebels took it over and emptied the fuel for themselves."

"No difference," Vincent said. "We've walked this far."

Sister Catherine stood at the door of the infirmary watching as they left.

It was very still. The trees were not moving. The forest was silent, waiting to swallow them. They heard a voice call out from behind. One of the nuns was running after them to hand them a package of food.

"You will be hungry later," she said.

Vincent looked back. Not just Sister Catherine, but the other nuns, the ones whose names he did not know, but Angeline did, were watching too.

CHAPTER TWENTY-THREE

Toward late afternoon they walked part of the way with a farmhand who called himself Motoumbe. He was dressed in gray slacks and a white button-down shirt, loose and hanging out of his pants, the cuffs undone, and a machete perched like an umbrella on his shoulder, the razor-sharp edge gleaming blue-white in the sunlight. Carrying it that way kept his hands free and swaying at his sides as he walked. He said he lived in a nearby village, earning his living working on one of the large farms, but it was dry season and the fields were barren; there would be no work for at least another month.

They walked along the path worn through the forest, talking a little here and there. Motoumbe did not seem to care who they were or why they were there. If anything he seemed grateful for the company.

"What about the proprietors?" Vincent asked. "Did they stay on?"

Motoumbe said, "The rebels frighten the *colons*. The owners are gone."

"In Pointe-Noire too?"

"In Pointe-Noire the *colons* feel safe. Too much money in Pointe-Noire to leave. Business as usual."

"You said there were farms near here. Where?" Vincent

asked. The idea that somewhere nearby were houses and farms seemed inconceivable.

"I can show you," Motoumbe said, stopping and pointing with his arm. "Twenty, maybe thirty trees in that direction, and you start to smell the difference. The trees smell of mahogany. You keep walking and you see there is a mahogany farm. The *colons* are gone. They take off the wheels and break up the machines before they go so no one steals the trees."

Motoumbe seemed intrigued by Angeline, and he looked at her without disguise. Then his thoughts shifted back to what must have been on his mind.

"When it's time to plant we see whether the *colons* come back. I think they will come back."

It surprised Vincent to hear Motoumbe speak of the owners returning.

"And what about the rebels, what happens when they come?" Vincent asked.

"Me? I am ready to fight for the rebels when they come." Motoumbe smiled as he said it, a generous smile that seemed out of place with what he was saying—with what they all knew it meant.

The inconsistency no longer bothered Vincent. For himself he would have made the choice: work for the *colons* or fight for the rebels. But he had begun to understand Motoumbe's way of thinking. For the people here it was a question of what opportunity presented itself.

They went their separate ways. Motoumbe was not going through the forest. He was heading toward his village in the opposite direction and they lost sight of him.

"They will all fight for the rebels," Angeline said.

She was not looking at Vincent. Instead she seemed to be thinking aloud, looking ahead onto the dirt path where

Motoumbe had disappeared.

"Do you blame them?" he asked.

Her eyes met his with a steady gaze, "The rebels are faithless, lawless bandits. Yet the rebels are their future," she said.

"No," he said. "Here there is no future. It never gets beyond the present. There is only today. How could it be otherwise when everyday you could die of thirst, hunger, insect bite or maybe a bullet or machete? And the odds never get better."

To himself he thought, if she loves it here, it's because she never wanted a future. She was watching him with her pale green eyes as if she could read his thoughts. He gazed softly back at her, I do not fault you; I've lived the same way, though he did not say it aloud.

The dry season was taking its toll; each day the terrain looked more parched than the day before. She stopped, broke a palm leaf off a dwarf palm tree with a rotten trunk and carried it in her hand, fanning herself as they walked.

Ahead of them was a forest of tall and fallen trees. The brush disappeared, choked out of existence by the roots of the enormous trees which stood like rows of kings before them, straight, majestic, stretching into the sky and leaving no doubt that the light at the top was heaven's light. The heat formed a heavy mist that filled in the spaces between trees.

Little gray monkeys with black faces and black eyes peered at them from the trees and made noises like laughter to call their attention.

"They are mocking us," she said.

"They are monkeys," he said. Yet the noise grated on him.

They came upon a large clearing. The trees had been cut down into stumps, evenly spaced like the headstones in a cemetery. Out of the shade the sun was scorching. There was a dirt road and there were tire tracks in the dirt that led to a clearing and a large house, open and flat, made of wood and stone and surrounded by a sparse grove of lemon trees, though the fruit had rotted and died. Only a small patch of wilting purple flowers growing close to the ground had somehow managed to survive. Angeline picked one and held it in the palm of her hand where it shriveled almost at once.

Someone had taken the trouble to cover the furniture with sheets before leaving. Motoumbe had been right, Vincent thought, the owners planned on returning. An enormous crystal chandelier, its dozen candles burnt at the top, hung from the ceiling of a large room that opened to the outdoors.

Angeline stood looking at it, smiling. "Can you imagine the trouble it took to get it here?"

On the far end of the room, there were two stone steps leading to a bedroom that opened onto a vegetable garden. Vincent followed Angeline outdoors. The temperature was dropping. The light had changed. Another hour before nightfall. Here it was beautiful and quiet after the racket of the forest, the sky still light but empty of the sun already resting on the horizon somewhere behind the trees where Pointe-Noire waited.

"I don't trust the forest at night," she said.

How could you? he thought. How could anyone? But there was something else that had nothing to do with the forest or magic or spirits stalking the wilderness. It was simpler than all of that. If he had not known before, he knew now, the truth is that we are desperate. We are born desperate and it never changes. All of our attempts to grab at life or to run away from it were driven by the same desperation. All or nothing.

"We could go on," he said, "then we're that much closer by morning."

"I want to spend the night with you here," she said.

He could not wait for the night. He carried her to the room with the chandelier and made love to her on the floor. The last rays of daylight were refracted in the prisms of crystal (*"Ice waiting to melt in the heat," she said*) her naked body draped in the shadows of dusk. She wrapped her warm arms around him and he felt her flesh against his.

"This is the last time," she whispered.

"The night is long here." (Hadn't she told him in Africa it is only possible to love at night?)

"If it is meant to last, it should be slow. *Doucement, chéri, doucement.*" She wrapped her hands gently behind his head. *"Doucement—"*

"I had forsaken gentleness, here where everything is extreme."

"You were always gentle to me," she said.

She guided him to her. Soon the light disappeared. It was dark when he held her again. Pulling her closer to him and bringing her mouth to his, he thought she is freer for loving because of it. He would have said her name aloud, told her he loved her, but he knew she would say the evil spirits are listening. Yet if they were he felt no trace of them.

"Everything around us is suffering, even the grass is dying.

As if we were in hell. Only the innocent are not supposed to be in hell, and here the victims are innocent."

"I have no answer," he said. Could he tell her what he felt—before her, love had not been possible? He held her tighter and buried his face in her hair. It was not yet dark enough to speak freely of love.

There was a well alongside the house with a shower nearby; she said she wanted to wash.

The floor was strewn with their clothes. She stepped over them on her way out. He stayed behind, feeling too spent to move. Even in the dark he could see the glint of the chandelier, a glimmer like stars in a distant sky. They had found cigarettes and bottles of French wine left behind. After a few minutes he got up and went out on the veranda to smoke. It was as if he had lived here his whole life. He could not imagine a different sky or a different sunset. He knew the weather; the heat during the day and the way the temperature dropped ten degrees at night but it felt like twenty because of the extreme heat of the day. He knew the shape of the hills, the hour of silence after nightfall before the night noises began and the way the stars cluttered the sky.

She brought candles to the table and lit them as she had that first night in her house when he was still weak from the fever—the first night of his life, he thought, nothing before counted. She was wearing a white shift, which she had found in an armoire in a bedroom, her skin and hair seeming so dark against the white. Her hair was wet and it hung below her waist. He wrapped his fingers around the round curve of her upper arm, the skin soft to the touch from washing.

"Look how it revived," she said. She was holding a cup with the purple flower she had picked from the front of the house. "They don't look it, but they are really very hardy."

"You have to be to survive here," he said.

He put out the cigarette and lifted her face in his hands. The dress was too big on her and it slipped from her shoulder.

He knew whatever she might do when they reached Pointe-Noire, her feelings for her husband were on the surface, like the lilies that grew atop the water, having nothing to do with what lay beneath.

It was very dark now, almost black, and the candlelight made long shadows against the walls of the house. He took her hand. This was the hand she had worn the wedding ring on. She seemed on the verge of saying something. He stopped her; she did not have to answer to him.

"I understand why you married him," he said. "It's a lonely place. You didn't want to be alone."

"Yes, but I was alone."

He stroked the long thin fingers. Better the hand is bare, he thought.

"Are my hands still cold?" she asked, as she wrapped her warm arms around his neck.

"Not tonight."

He opened the bottle of wine with a knife. When they drank they had to pick the pieces of cork out. French wine instead of palm wine, red and very rich. It went to his head.

"To our honeymoon," he said only half ironically.

He remembered being angry with his mother, begging her with tears in his eyes not to die. Anger, tears, they are nothing. She died and there was that lesson to be learned, the lesson he learned early in life—isn't it what Angeline had meant when she said the evil spirits are listening? Love anything and it dies. He would not ask her to go on with him after Pointe-Noire.

"What do you think? We'll walk into town and a band will start playing?" She was laughing, a giddy drunken laugh.

"I think it will be nothing," he said. "We will have arrived, that's all."

They should have slept, but they did not want to sleep. They sat out on the veranda until they had finished the bottle of wine. The sky was full of stars and it seemed to him as if they had been given this glimpse of heaven having been through hell first.

"There is a bed," she said at last, taking his hand.

He shook his head.

"You don't like beds?" she teased.

"It's the mattress. You can get AIDS from bedbugs."

She took his hand and led him to the room with the chandelier. "Like sleeping beneath the stars," she said.

To please her he lit the candles, and the light came alive from above, the flames trembling in the still air as shadows streaked the wall. In the warm glow of light he saw her pale eyes, gazing hard at him. There was a quality of despair in that look, and he wanted to tell her, no matter what happens when they reach Pointe-Noire, she should not despair.

He brought her mouth to his and kissed her, desiring her the way a dream repeats itself.

"This is good-bye," she said.

"Do you love me?" he asked.

She continued to gaze at him, but the hardness had gone from her stare, and with it the despair too. He held her shoulders in his hands.

"Do you love me?" he repeated, and he held her tighter.

"Yes. Kiss me," she said, and he did, breathlessly, savagely, no longer believing it would end.

CHAPTER TWENTY-FOUR

It was a deep, heavy sleep because of the wine. Her hair was lying across his face and he pushed it off. He saw the chandelier with the candles burnt to the wick. His back was stiff and he felt a terrible thirst that he quenched with water. He left her sleeping and went out onto the veranda. It was very early in the morning. The night had already faded from the sky. The air was damp, the way it is before dawn, and he felt a chill.

He boiled water for tea. Then he smoked. Not long after, the sun came up. He watched the sky turn red as he drank the hot tea. An animal let out a cry across the new day. He understood why she believed in sorcerers and fetishes; there was magic in those colored dawns—beauty too, but with it indifference, and even cruelty.

He thought of the first time he saw her, the angel's face appearing through the delirium of fever. Now his thoughts were so clear: he had wasted so much time. Before her he had not lived his life, but had allowed himself to be drawn along as if by the current in a river, nothing to lose, nothing to gain, just life passing through him. It was different now. Because of her there was something at stake.

The shift she had been wearing was on the floor next to her. She was sleeping, her face lovely and sad, her arm had slipped free of the blanket, and he bent down and gently covered her. That first night when he asked her why she stayed, she told him, "Everything I know is here." Would she say it again today if he asked her? Good-bye to this place, the beautiful dawns and colored sunsets, green hills, the bush, the slow-moving rivers, all surfaces that deceived—good-bye to Africa, all of it. She opened her eyes for a moment, then like a sleeping child fell back to sleep.

The air was already warm. What he wanted was a shower and he went out back to where the pump was behind the house. The water was very cold; it felt good, all that cold water washing away the heat and the dust, and he remained for a few minutes with the cold water running over him. Afterward, he dressed quickly. He had started toward the house when he heard a noise that caused him to look back. He saw the sun first, blaring in the sky. A moment after he saw the gun pointed at his head.

He recognized Motoumbe at once. He was wearing the same clothes as yesterday, but his friendly expression was now menacing. There were six of them all together, a rebel death squad. They dressed in whatever they had. There was no need for a uniform. He knew by the mad look in their faces who they were.

They were all pointing assault rifles at his head. He took it in like a breath. His body went stiff. He did not speak or move. He knew if he resisted he was a dead man.

He was unsure of what they wanted. Yet he could tell from their hesitation they too were unsure. For a split instant the thought of Angeline sleeping in the house flashed across his mind. But even a thought is dangerous in this situation.

He shielded his gaze by looking at them through lowered eyelids. The barrels of their guns were so close he could smell the metal and bitter residue of gunpowder along with the odor of beer and sweat. Motoumbe, though silent, appeared pleased with himself for having led the death squad there.

One of them took his gun.

"Take off your clothes," the leader of the squad stepped forward and commanded him, jabbing the end of his rifle into his ribs. The leader was young, like the others, closer to twenty than thirty. He was almost Vincent's exact height. For a moment their eyes met at close range, Vincent's dead stare and the other with the mad look.

"Take off your clothes," he repeated.

Vincent undressed. Cold from the shower, he fought to prevent himself from shivering; they would have taken it as fear and been excited by it.

"Down on your knees."

Vincent went on his knees and someone bound his hands behind his back; he felt the callused, sweaty hands pulling and twisting at his wrists; the knot was tied too tight and it cut off the circulation.

"There is a woman with you. Call her," the leader said.

The others were silent, always silent, staring at him with hard eyes or behind sunglasses; only the leader spoke.

Vincent did not answer. He felt the gun jab deeper into his ribs. The sun was burning his eyes.

Now time was nothing, every second a lifetime in which his life was to be spared or taken—*Angeline*, he thought again to himself. They have not found her.

"Call her."

He felt a blow to the back of his head and a pain in his

skull. He caught his breath. There was a second blow, which knocked him forward. He thought he was going to faint. When he tried to get up, he could not; he felt too tired. He could smell the gun and the sweat of the man leaning over him and he tried to open his eyes. Then he felt a third blow on the side of his head, his teeth knocked together and he blacked out.

When he came to the pain was awful. The side of his head was burning as if his head had caught fire. He was on the ground, lying on his back. He could feel the sweat drenching his body, mixing with the blood, a putrid sour taste on his lips. Someone dressed in a black tee shirt and army fatigues with a black scarf wrapped tight around his head was bent over him. He had a thin face and long features.

"We know the woman is with you."

It was the leader who spoke, but Vincent could not see him. Blood ran down his face. He turned his head to try to prevent it from dripping across his eye.

"You are a spy for the government."

This time he answered.

"I am Lieutenant Vincent Chavanne. My mission is to evacuate French nationals on behalf of France," realizing as he said it that he had probably spoken his name—heard it aloud—for the last time.

"The French have left. You are a collaborator." The leader hung on the word collaborator, caressing each syllable with his tongue.

Dizzy with pain and loss of blood, the idea seemed ludicrous to him.

The one with the thin face stepped back in deference to the leader who bent down to touch Vincent's face with his long brown fingers. Vincent could smell the alcohol on his breath, even through the sour smell of his own blood. Why is he touching my face like that, he wondered, struggling against the weakness he felt and the wish to close his eyes and be done with it.

The leader dipped his fingers into the wet blood dripping down Vincent's face, bringing it to his nostrils as if he were inhaling it. He signaled to one who looked like a boy, too small to wear the *Kalashnikov* on his shoulder; he had to put it down in the dirt to take a small knife from his pocket. The leader stood to the side as the boy sliced Vincent's skin, a long diagonal cut from the shoulder across the chest just deep enough for the blood to pour out.

They all came, one by one. They painted their faces with his fresh blood. When it was Motoumbe's turn Vincent looked straight at him. Motoumbe's eyes were bloodshot and glazed over as if he had never seen Vincent before today.

"Where is the woman?" the leader repeated, hitting him across the side of the head with the blunt end of his automatic.

Vincent let out a cry. His hair was black with perspiration and his face as pale as ivory. Though sweat was flooding his body, inside he felt cold, as if he were about to freeze to death.

"You think her pussy only tastes good in your mouth. We want some too," the leader said.

The idea occurred to him that they had been close the whole time, like hunters, waiting for the kill, savoring it. But no, it could not be. It was just bad luck meeting Motoumbe on the road.

It seemed they let him be for a while, giving the pain time

to mount. He knew himself it was more effective that way—the pain would grow and with it the desire to live, the respite from beating and torture would yield way to the human instinct to live, then one would say anything, do anything—

His left eye was covered with blood and he could no longer see out of it. They were playing a game. It was fun to beat him, because blood is a drug like alcohol or hashish. People who have been in battle know it; the smell of blood is addictive.

Through one eye he watched the sky, the blue was being overtaken by heavy white clouds that hung just above the tops of the sky, and beyond the clouds it was blue, deep menacing blue like water. His head was burning. He wondered how much longer until they shot him. What would happen to Angeline? If they had not found her, there was a chance she might have escaped. These thoughts took an effort that was beyond him. Fresh blood began to drip from the wound in his head. He looked up at the sky again: it was too large, too close, there was no peace in that blue, no softening of the light from behind the clouds, only the sun threatening…

"Stand up."

He was too weak to stand on his own. Motoumbe and one other lifted him to his feet and supported him, their sweating bodies pressing against his. They were soaked in sweat and his blood was running down their necks and arms. The tallest of the six stood in front of him with his machete, glaring through mad eyes. Then he swung the blunt end of the machete and crushed both of Vincent's knees in a blow.

He let out a loud cry as his body gave way beneath him. He thought he was going to fall over, faint and die, but they held him up. The tall man stepped aside. It was the leader again, standing before him, his gun poised. He fired two shots into his thigh and the bullets shattered his femur. They let go supporting him, and he collapsed, the piercing shriek he could no longer suppress raging across the bush.

There was talk of whether he should be taken as a hostage.

The boy who had cut him with the machete pointed his gun and said he wanted to shoot him.

"He will die in a few hours."

The leader turned to Vincent, grinning, "We will kill the woman when she comes back for you."

Then he motioned with his rifle and the death squad disappeared as swiftly as they had come.

CHAPTER TWENTY-FIVE

The sun woke her, shining in her eyes through the open doors. She glanced around her, looking for Vincent. He must have gone outdoors, she thought. Yet that did not account for the empty feeling in the room, more so than yesterday, as if she had been alone for a long time.

The rest seemed like a dream. She seemed to see them before they appeared, like a breeze blowing through the trees, everything seemed to stir, but the air was still, the jeep suddenly driving up out of nowhere, and the death squad jumping out, weapons pointed. Then she started to run, running without looking back. She kept running, past the equipment sheds because they would look for her there, into the trees, which somehow she knew would protect her. Everything was dry. She heard the brittle leaves cracking beneath her feet as she ran. Then she stopped and crouched close to the ground. From where she was she could see the house; it seemed to tremble.

She could not see what was happening. Yet she knew the cry of agony, which at first did not sound human, was coming from Vincent, and with each cry, she wanted to run to him. But fear paralyzed her, as if she had forgotten how to move her arms and legs. Get up, get up, she repeated the words and yet she remained. She knew the awful truth; there was nothing she could do for him now. To help him she had to wait until they were gone.

After a silence that seemed too long two shots were fired, and through the cries of the birds as they took to the air, she heard a final piercing shriek. They are murdering him, she thought.

In the dreadful silence that accompanied the last scream, she feared it was too late; he was already dead.

She felt the *nkisi* hanging from her neck, pinching her skin.

It was you, Marguerite— you saved me, you woke me and showed me the way out of there. And not him? You did not warn him. You could have saved him and you did not. Why?

She knew the answer. She pictured the forlorn face of the old *féticheuse*, the muscles in her long thin arms strained to the point of exhaustion, because love of any kind is a burden. *Who am I to go against what God wishes?*

The torpid air had a strange smell of dead leaves and gasoline. The birds had begun to squawk again. They were deep in the branches of the trees and they seemed excited and louder than before. She heard the engine starting up, but she did not wait until they were out of sight before she ran to him.

When Vincent saw her, a smile, heartbreaking for its sadness, passed over his pale lips.

"You're alive," she cried, and her eyes filled with tears at the sight of his naked and broken body. He lay like an inert mass in a pool of his own blood, his beautiful face marred by blood and swelling. The left eye was closed; the other did not move. His legs were disfigured and swollen. She saw the long gash across his chest.

Kneeling beside him, she undid the rope around his wrists. His lips parted on the verge of saying something, but the pain that ran through his body at that moment prevented him.

She bent closer to him and clasped his face in her hands. "My God, what have they done to you? Do not die, Vincent, please do not die."

The chill of death had already entered him and he knew he was going to die. He knew at last why his mother had complained of being cold. Death is a coldness that enters under the skin.

He did not tell her he was dying, as she tried to restrain her tears, but she did not need him to tell her. Death had already won over, and he was aloof, gazing silently at her through distant eyes.

She, almost lifeless from despair, placed a kiss on his brow, just above his eyes.

"Your beautiful eyes," she said with tenderness. She saw the life draining from them.

"I have been looking at you," he said. And as he looked at her, he hated death for what he was going to lose.

The pain intensified and left him weakened, and in his anguish he stopped seeing her next to him. There was a dimness in his eyes that covered over everything. There was no mystery left to his life. He knew its shape, all its contours had been revealed, without a future, only a present that was rapidly draining from him. He was not frightened of God, neither of God nor of death; he thought of the two in the same breath. The pain he felt made death desirable, as desirable as ending the torment, and he was ready to succumb.

"I'm sorry," she whispered, her face bent over his hand, kissing it lightly. "I kept running. I didn't come back for you."

"You had to run. They would have killed you. Nothing could have made a difference." To himself he thought, God Himself would have had to come and He did not.

"It was me who wanted to stay the night here," she said in a broken voice. "We would have been gone this morning when they came."

Her hair fell over her shoulder and brushed his face as she bent closer to him and touched her lips against his cheek.

"I wanted to stay too—as much as you, more—"

He made an effort to kiss her and tasted the bitter savor of her tears across his lips, a reminder that his concerns for life were not over: he had to make sure she escaped before they came back.

"You have to go," he said. "They expect you to come back for me."

"The rebels are gone," she said, her eyes brimming with despair that was palpable.

"Temporarily, to trap you. They will come for you. They said it. Believe me, otherwise they would have killed me on the spot."

"Let them come. I'm not afraid—not with you."

He pressed her hand. "You are so close to Pointe-Noire," he said. "I promised I would take you to Pointe-Noire." His voice was so weak she could scarcely make out the words.

"Go."

"Only if you come with me," she said in a broken whisper. "I'm not leaving you here."

"My legs are crushed. It's impossible. There is nothing that can be done for me."

She leaned her face close to his. He felt the warmth of her tears and placed his mouth against hers, her soft lips comforting him, for a moment making death seem terrible again because it would take her from him, her talking eyes that spoke to him without words, the scent of jasmine on her skin when he kissed her, no more, only tears and blood. Her tears were stained with his blood across her face, and he raised his fingers to her cheek to wipe them. His assassins had streaked their faces with his blood—hatred, contempt and yet to see that symbol erased by another, the look of her eyes, tears of sorrow and love. Tomorrow and the day after were no longer of interest to him. At the moment of his death he would love her.

"You were right. Here it is unto death."

It had become a very hot and humid afternoon. There was no shade; the palm trees were dying, the large brown leaves hanging lifeless.

She brought him water, which he drank from her cupped hands. He seemed very distant. He would not look at her now. She tore her shift into pieces to wash him. The flies had gathered in the wound on his head, which, after cleaning as best she could, she wrapped with a strip of cloth. She was afraid to leave him—not even for as long as it would take to get a fresh cloth from the house. She washed the blood from his face; he was white as a ghost and sweating profusely though he trembled as if he had chills. The bullet in his thigh was wedged deep in the bone. No matter how she washed and bandaged the opening, the bleeding did not stop. When she touched the area, he shrieked with pain. Every time he moved was an agony.

"Calme-toi, calme-toi," her voice breaking as she whispered.

Though his eyes remained in semi-darkness, he saw her in his mind as clearly as if he were watching her, the infant cradled in her arms, her voice, like the purring of a cat, soothing and gentle... *Calme-toi.*

She found his clothes in the dirt, they had left them, but his boots had been stolen—a detail, a pair of boots looted by bandits. One of them was undoubtedly wearing them now. And yet when she saw his boots were gone, she cried.

Taking his shirt, she opened it and placed it over his chest. Any more of an attempt at dressing him would have been impossible—even the feel of the cloth against his skin as she washed him was too painful for him. She clasped his hand, which rested weakly inside hers.

"I love you," she whispered.

He opened his eyes and his weak gaze met hers. The swelling in his head was getting worse. Then it was as if he were sleeping; his eyes did not open.

For a while she considered whether she could get somewhere—if not Pointe-Noire, the shantytowns outside, in time to get medical attention.

He slipped into a coma. She knew he would not awaken. He was going to die from the injury to his skull. All hope of leaving him to go for help was abandoned.

She lifted him by placing her arms under his and, as gently as she could, half-dragged, half-pulled his limp body inside the house. She was trembling and exhausted from exertion, but she felt nothing; everything had gone numb inside of her and she was disconnected from the ordeals of her body. The room where they had slept together the night before was nearest, and she struggled to bring him there, the large, empty room with only the chandelier suspended like heaven itself above their heads—the death squad had broken it to pieces and ripped it from the ceiling. Crystals were scattered across the floor, and the sunlight was reflected in shattered prisms of light as if the stars had fallen from the sky. It was unbearable to see him lying amidst the debris on the hard floor, so she made a bed for him from a torn mattress that she dragged from a bedroom.

She went back outside and filled a basin with water to use during the night. The moon, which had been stalking them all those nights, keeping watch over their movements, was at last full and beaming its cold selenium light over the ground as she walked back toward the house.

All night she lay beside him in the dark, listening for his breath, wiping the flies from his face, moistening his lips with water. From time to time she closed her eyes, but she was never near to sleep. She went to the window as the silhouette of the trees began to emerge from the night. Earth and sky were again separate, the finite and the eternal. Rays of sunlight like the fingers of God lifted the remnants of night from the sky. There was nothing left.

"Adieu, my love, not good-bye, but adieu—to God."

She buried her head in her hands and fell to her knees sobbing.

He had died during the night. She had been next to him, clasping his hand. She heard him gasp for air, and she brought him to her breast and held him as the spirit left the body.

She wanted to see him a last time in the light, waiting until light filled the room before she covered him with a sheet. She did not kiss his eyes after she closed them, nor his lips— the stillness of death was too much to bear in those places, but buried her kiss deep into his forehead, as if to leave the imprint of her soul through eternity.

She took the *nkisi* from her neck and placed it inside his still hand. It occurred to her that she had nothing to remember him by, no photograph, nothing with his name on it. Even the clothes he had worn were not his. She picked up a piece of crystal from the broken chandelier, a fallen star, she thought. They had been together in this room and this fragment of heaven was what remained of that night.

She lingered for a long time without knowing why. Then she realized she was waiting for the death squad to return, but they did not.

CHAPTER TWENTY-SIX

The birds were singing in the trees. The day was beginning like any other. The air was already thick and she could feel the sun burning the clouds from the sky. The grass was tall and so dry it had no color, neither burnt yellow nor gold, but a color that reminded her of death.

By afternoon she passed the shantytown outside of Pointe-Noire. The inhabitants stood along the road, mostly women and children since the men worked in the mines or oil rigs in Pointe-Noire. Her presence was so unlikely in a countryside where all the whites had left or were hiding that they took her for the embodiment of a malevolent spirit. Her skin was dry and covered in a thin layer of chalk because she was too dehydrated to sweat. The absence of sweat especially frightened the women. "Zombie, zombie," they shrieked as she passed. They could smell death on her skin, and they grabbed their children and ran back to the town where they closed the doors to their houses. They saw what she did not; the spirit of the dead man walking beside her.

A truck passed her along the road. When she first heard it, she thought, now they will kill me, and it will be done. The dust from the tires blew in her nose and eyes, but the truck did not stop. As it drove by she saw it was an old Berliot filled to the brim with passengers.

There was an army checkpoint halfway between the shantytown and Pointe-Noire. She was spotted from a distance. The captain approached her with two soldiers at his side. Studying her from beneath his hat and black sunglasses, he was about to ask her for her papers when her legs gave way beneath her and she fainted.

She was driven the rest of the way to Pointe-Noire in a truck. She woke up in the back of the truck, shivering despite the afternoon heat. There were Congolese soldiers watching her with expressions of sullen indifference. She felt as if she were struggling to awaken from a dream at the moment in the dream when something terrible is about to happen. But there was no waking up. Then it was a different feeling, as if she were passing between two worlds, her world with Vincent and the world to which she was returning, and the two worlds were irreconcilable; there was no place for her in either one. Looking up, the sky was a peaceful blue. She curled her legs closer to her chest as the truck bounced across the uneven road to Pointe-Noire.

It was truly a different world inside Pointe-Noire. The sidewalks were full, workers, schoolchildren, women doing errands with babies strapped to their backs, lines of taxis so full they could scarcely move, their wheels scraping the broken pavement under the weight, and the air thick with the smell of gasoline as dense as the haze. It was a characteristic of all the African cities she had known, day or night—people were always outdoors except when the city was at war. There was no sign of war in Pointe-Noire. She noticed at once. No one in Pointe-Noire was thinking about war.

They headed down the Avenue de Gaulle, the soldiers pointing their guns from the back of the truck to stop traffic so the truck could pass. She was taken to the French Consulate. The captain stayed behind to talk to a soldier inside the entrance hall as she was escorted to a room with a bed where she could rest, a small yellowed room with a ceiling fan that no one had turned on and a few pieces of furniture, a silk brocade chair, an old fauteuil that seemed to have been left there for want of a better place.

After a few minutes the Vice-Consul came to see her, a portly, middle-aged man with dark silver hair and puffy features. He seemed very tired, she thought, something more than the insomnia of the tropics, a resignation that went deep beneath the skin. He pulled the fauteuil closer to the bed; she could smell the cigarette he had just finished smoking still in his hands and on his breath.

"We have been looking for you," he said in a soft-spoken voice.

"If you were looking for me, you would have found me," she answered.

There was a long window over the bed with a view of the street. She opened the shutters and looked out. The sweet smell of frying bananas was as heavy as the air. It stuck in her nostrils and in her throat. A woman hung laundry out a nearby window. Cars were honking their horns; a taxi had broken down in the street in front of the Consulate and a crowd of men had gathered.

"Your husband is in Gabon. The military closed the borders and he could not get back into the Congo. We're making arrangements now."

"The whites have stayed in Pointe-Noire," she said, turning

her gaze back to the Vice-Consul. She had seen white people on the street when she arrived.

"Evacuation has not been required here. People were given the choice. The oil workers sent their families home and stayed on themselves."

She turned away from the window.

"Does Patrick know what happened?"

"About the plantation, yes."

Thought of Patrick struck a chord inside of her. She imagined the flurry of phone calls and faxes as he tried to find out what had happened. And then the solution, what he was best at. He could get things done, something she had always admired about him. She pictured him holding the cigarette between his fingers, his straight black hair falling to the side, his steel blue eyes and his pale complexion, like Belgian cream despite living in the tropics.

But she had not come to Pointe-Noire for Patrick. Their marriage now seemed intolerable to her, an empty space, a void that could never be filled between them.

"Since the attack on my property I have been traveling with Lt. Vincent Chavanne, who was assassinated yesterday by a rebel death squad," she said. The sound of Vincent's name awakened her from numbness and her voice faltered as she continued. "His body remains at the main house of a mahogany plantation some hours walking distance east of Pointe-Noire." She could not be more precise, yet she knew even so they would be able to find it.

What she had said, however, took the diplomat by surprise, and some mix of excitement and horror broke through his tired eyes. "Lt. Chavanne has been missing in action. How was he with you?"

She did not hear his question. "We would have both made it to Pointe-Noire if only—." Her voice trembled and she turned her face back to the window. She did not say it aloud, but to herself: We made a mistake believing there was time for tenderness; we forgot where we were.

A medic came to examine her.

"You are dehydrated," he said.

He placed a tray with a pitcher and a small glass on the table beside her bed.

"You must drink, small sips at first, every few minutes for the first hour, then you can try drinking more at a time."

From the bed she could see a French soldier waiting outside the doorway, dressed in uniform, wearing the *képi noir* over his cropped hair. He glanced into the room and caught her eye for an instant, then leaned back against the wall and continued waiting. When the medic left, he stood in the doorway.

"May I come in?" he asked.

"Who are you?" she asked weakly, without lifting herself from the bed.

"Lt. Bernard Simone."

Simone stepped into the sallow light of the room.

"Vincent was my friend," he said.

With this she sat up. "Come closer," she said.

He positioned a chair beside the bed. He filled the glass from the pitcher and handed it to her.

"The medic said you should drink."

She brought the glass to her lips and sipped, but her eyes never left Simone's face. Simone, however, his head bowed, seemed lost in thought, strangely unaware of her presence.

He folded his hands in front of him into a fist and shook his head. He had to clear his throat before he could speak.

"I have been going over things in my mind. There were three soldiers with Vincent when the jeep was attacked. Their bodies were recovered. Only Vincent was missing. We went out in Brazzaville looking for anyone with information. People there took me to a girl who witnessed the explosion. She said she saw a French soldier on the ground and the body of a rebel on top of him. They were looting the bodies, taking whatever they could. She brought me to the boys who were doing the looting. One of them had Vincent's watch."

Angeline could not see Simone's eyes beneath the brim of the *képi*, only the sweat glistening along the sides of his face.

He reached into his pocket and held out the watch, a Breitling with a black face and black leather band, leaving Angeline to imagine how he had gotten it back. Fingering the leather band as he spoke, he said, "I saw the boy—he was old enough to tell the difference between alive and dead." His voice rose slightly and he raised his eyes to meet hers. "He said he was dead. He had to have felt his wrist when he took the watch. We recovered the other bodies. Everyone we spoke to said there were no living. We waited. We continued to make inquiries. It was expected that if Vincent were alive he would have been taken hostage and the rebels would have made a ransom demand. The situation in the area was volatile and more casualties were feared. After a few days we were ordered to give up the search. Headquarters would not clear us to go into the jungle to look for a dead body."

When he was finished, he handed the watch to Angeline, "I should have known. There was no body. I should have gone on looking. I shouldn't have given up."

Angeline clutched the watch in her palm as a picture of Vincent emerged in her mind, clean-shaven, dressed in his uniform—the way he had looked in her dream, standing by the window veiled behind the sheer white drape. At last she knew why in the dream he was crying. She closed her hand.

"I would like to make arrangements for him to be buried with his mother," Angeline said, her voice so composed it concealed her grief. "He told me he was from Marseilles."

Lt. Simone looked up. "I will notify the administration and they will take care of the rest."

She lowered her eyes and looked down at the watch, which was damp with the moisture of her palm. Simone had been his friend. The man who had worn this watch—Simone could tell her—the nights they had gotten drunk together, the things they talked about, laughed about, the small things as well as the big, especially the small things. How many years had they been friends? Ten? Maybe more? Compared to the ten days she and Vincent had together. Maybe what she felt for him and what she believed he felt for her was nothing, the part of the nightmare that wraps the wish inside of it. If he were here sitting next to Simone, soldiers in uniform, could she say she knew him?

The afternoon sun streaked across the yellow walls. She felt unsure of herself and of what she felt. Then she remembered the broken piece of chandelier; it was in her pocket. "I took it from the room where he died," she said, showing it to Simone, though she did not explain any further. As she held it in her open hand, the fading sunlight filled it with color, a prism of light beating in her hand, and watching it, she stopped doubting herself. What more did she need to know? Her love for Vincent was complete, a moment in time, like light through glass.

She heard the loud noise of the fan spinning; Simone had turned it on. The warm air was circulating in a rough breeze.

She lifted her eyes to meet his. "You should keep this," she said, holding the watch. "It belongs to you now."

He hesitated, but she reached out her hand and gave it to him. "You will remember him by it," she said.

CHAPTER TWENTY-SEVEN

Patrick arrived that night. When he came into the room he found her lying on the narrow bed, her head buried in her arms, neither asleep nor quite awake either.

"I have been trying to get back in the country," he said in a gentle voice, seeming unsure of what she was feeling.

"Patrick," she started and lifted her head, her voice was hoarse and scarcely recognizable and her pale green eyes were swollen from crying.

He seemed to want to embrace her, but he felt her distance and he held back, approaching her tentatively, seating himself beside her on the bed and holding out his hands, waiting for her to accept his gesture. She sat up and resting her head against his shoulder, she began to cry silently.

"I blame myself for having been away, and then when I tried to get back, everywhere I turned there was a wall," he said softly, close to her ear, so she could feel his voice trembling against her skin.

He took her limp hands in his, and clasped them tight. After a moment she felt him stroke the bare space on her finger where she had worn her wedding band. He did not need to say anything for her to know what he was asking. "I gave it away in exchange for a piece of cloth, a rag, in fact." Seeking out his gaze, she said in a quiet voice. "Do not expect any-thing from me, Patrick," and he gently let go.

Gentle—the word to describe how they were to one an-other, exchanging glances through the gray light of the room where the street noises were muffled by the churning of the fan. The night, which had settled in without their noticing, seemed to offer no respite from the heat of the day.

She felt weak again and lay on the bed. He sat across from her, feeling in the way, like an intruder. "I won't ask you to tell me what you've been through," he said. Looking at her he saw for himself; she was thin, very thin, and her eyes seemed larger, deeper because of what they had seen, an ex-pression that was both sorrow and pity, and yet there was warmth in those eyes, and love.

The window was open wide, and after a while he went over to have a look. In contrast to the silence of the room, there was the welcome distraction of the noisy street, music blaring from open-air bars, voices, laughter.

He remained looking out the window until someone came in with tea. Angeline poured out a cup.

"None for you?" she asked.

He shook his head. "It's too hot. Maybe a Coke."

She sat up to drink and he seemed to welcome this op-portunity to talk to her.

"I've made arrangements for us to take an apartment in Paris for now," he said. "In a few months I can arrange for us to live in Gabon."

"I won't come back to Africa." She shook her head and smiled slightly. "I have lived my life here. Everything that belonged to me, everything I cared about was here. When I leave I will have nothing, not even a valise."

Patrick lit a cigarette. The fan took up the heavy smoke and the smell of French tobacco hung in the air.

"The government maintains the rebels will not come as far as Pointe-Noire. They're mistaken." He exhaled before continuing. "France is backing the rebels because of the oil contract the government made with the Americans."

At the time he said it, he had not expected her to have a reaction—a question of politics—nothing more. But he saw the change that overcame her face. He took the teacup from her hand; she was shaking too much to hold it, and the hot tea spilled on her thigh. She scarcely noticed. For a moment her thoughts faltered. Then she thought of Vincent, the terrible pain he felt during those final hours.

"The French were backing the rebels." She repeated it aloud and an anguished sigh escaped from her lips.

The Vice-Consul had told Patrick the French soldier who had accompanied her was murdered by rebels.

"Whether he was French or a soldier meant nothing to them. They murdered him because he was white," Patrick said.

He tried to comfort her in his arms, but he knew at once he had made a mistake, and in the next moment he knew the magnitude of the mistake. She communicated with her body what she did not put in words: she had been in love with Lt. Chavanne. He understood now—the look in her eyes, her languid body, the day and night of crying—he recognized it for what it was.

The long ash fell from his cigarette and he ground it into the wood floor with his heel.

She hid her face in her hands rather than look at him. He could hear her sobbing, yet she had made clear there was nothing he could do for her. After a few minutes, he left, quietly closing the door behind him.

The sound of the door was a relief to her. She wanted to be alone to mourn the loss of what had been the deepest love of her life. She lay in bed, her face buried in the cushion, thinking of Vincent, envisioning his face in detail—the way his warm smile took over his eyes—but the image of his death would not go away, and memory was interrupted by tears like a mirror that kept shattering each time she looked. Too soon to remember him, she thought, she loved him as if he were alive. The night before last he had held her in his arms as they slept. How could it be that she was here, inside the Consulate, and he was not?

Grief kept her from sleeping. Sometime during the night there was a knock at the door. She assumed it was Patrick. Instead, a soldier in uniform stood in the doorway like an apparition. She focused her eyes through her tears and recognized Lt. Simone.

"We have brought him back," he said.

He approached, and in the light of the small bedside lamp she could see into his sharp brown eyes.

"Vincent was holding this in his hand when we found him," he said, holding out the *nkisi* for her to see.

She spoke without looking up or taking her eyes from the deformed little object or the warm, sweating palm that held it. "It's a nail fetish; you pierce it when you are afraid of something—it was mine and I left it with him." She paused as if to think, "A silly child's charm, that's all."

She gazed through the hazy light at Simone. "Vincent was not afraid. He was courageous and strong and good. You saw him. You know how he suffered."

The sight of his friend's brutalized corpse had unbalanced Simone.

"He was a hero," he said, his voice breaking up as he said it.

At the airport there was a small military ceremony before the casket, draped in the French flag, was carried onto the plane by six Legionnaires, Lt. Simone among them. Angeline stood beside Patrick. Her back was straight. There were no tears. What she felt at that moment remained hidden behind the dark glasses she wore.

Patrick asked her if she wanted him to accompany her to Marseilles for the funeral. She said she wanted to be alone.

It began to rain suddenly, a heavy, tropical rain, delaying the flight until it stopped ten minutes later, like a faucet that was turned off. Steam rose from the tarmac. Angeline watched the sky as the last clouds dispersed, leaving the sky a gray, brooding blue, the color of Vincent's eyes, she thought, and she felt him surrounding her like a dream.

Patrick gently took her hand.

"It's time to go," he said.

On October 15, 1997, the Cobra militia captured Brazzaville and Pointe-Noire, which surrendered without a fight. The four-month civil war was ended as rebel forces of the former Marxist leader Denis Sassou Nguesso proclaimed victory.

The morning I met Bill Packard it was warm, still summery. I remember the gentle blue sky, the mellow sunlight and the late September smell of dry leaves. The sidewalk was empty. It was a quiet Sunday morning in the West Village as I walked down Eighth Avenue to HB Studios, my first autumn in the city in many years.

I must have read about HB studios in the *Village Voice*. When I went there someone in the office advised me to sign up for William Packard's Sunday morning playwriting class.

Somehow the walk to HB that Sunday morning was more memorable than the class itself. What I do remember is going up to Bill at the end of the class and handing him my resume. Looking back, it seems like an odd thing to have done. It did serve one purpose: when I did not return the following week, Bill called me.

I think of the lines from Pascal that Bill loved and often repeated to me in that breathless way he had of reading as if he were lying in the dark imagining the light. "You would not have looked for me if you had not already found me." So it was, in searching I found Bill.

He offered to take a look at two short plays I had written during my last year at law school. I went to his apartment the following Saturday afternoon. Recently, I described my first visit to Bill's apartment to a few friends who did not know him in those days. They were astonished by my description of a university professor's apartment, clean, neatly organized, with handsome wooden furniture, walls of bookshelves, artwork and plenty of light from the windows. I remember sitting at the polished wooden table in the center of the main room. Alongside the table on a stand was a large black and white photograph of a pretty young woman with blonde hair and an expression, a little sad, a little anguished, and yet as I think back on it I remember she was smiling.

The only thing Bill said about her that afternoon was that he had taken the picture. When I got to know him better he told me a lot about her. She was still very much a part of his life in those days. She would show up at his door in the middle of the night after a self-destructive rampage. When she killed herself she dug a hole in his heart that was never repaired. He could not say her name without his voice breaking. A time would come years later when he stopped talking about her. Yet he told her story over and over; every girl in every play he wrote had a piece of her in it.

It was after her death that he turned his gaze away from the future to the past. He began the autobiography, and with it the story of his mother who authorized the lobotomy that was performed on his father. The neat professor's apartment began to decline into clutter and dust and as the years passed black soot on the windows blocked the light. He no longer noticed.

He reduced his life to the things that truly mattered to him—"the writing", "the magazine" and "the teaching." In the interstices there was black coffee, cigarettes and Village coffee shops. During this period he published several books, among them the successful craft books on poetry and screenwriting. He kept *The New York Quarterly*, the poetry magazine that he founded, alive against the odds. But throughout, he continued to write what he referred to as, "The Autobiography." If it had another title I never knew it.

He spent ten years writing "The Autobiography." The catharsis he appeared to be seeking drained him. Within days of finishing the manuscript, he fell to the floor with a small stroke. There were to be no lasting consequences from the stroke. But it was the first sign that his health was deteriorating.

In the winter of 1994 he slipped during a snowstorm and broke his leg so badly he needed three surgeries and spent the winter in St. Vincent's Hospital. He almost died of an infection. But as he often said of himself, "I am a tough son of a bitch." He was.

He recovered and by the summer he was teaching again. It appeared those months in the hospital had served to heal more than the broken leg. Teaching had taken on a new vitality. He added a few classes. His writing was going well too. His plays were being performed regularly. The years he had spent grieving for the girl who committed suicide, for the father who had been lobotomized, for the son he had given up all rights to when he was still too young to know what it was he was giving up had passed. He seemed to be looking toward the future.

We met for a coffee on a Sunday evening. I saw him on the street corner as I approached, leaning on his wooden cane with the carved handle, wearing the same golden-brown corduroy jacket that he had been wearing winter or summer since I met him, the pockets weighed down with agendas and writing books, tape recorders and fountain pens. He seemed strong and handsome, the corners of his mouth turned up in a smile. In his hand he had a red silk rose that he handed to me for Mother's Day.

Two years later he made a video of my daughter playing in the park for her birthday. After a while he handed me the camera and asked me to film him. In what was at best a fleeting glimpse, a shy gaze that too quickly turned away from its subject, I focused the camera on him for an instant and gave it back.

Only a few days later he suffered a stroke and he would never stand on his own again.

It was after the stroke, when he was at the Terence Cardinal Cooke Health Center, that I first began talking to him about *Soldier in the Grass*. It was a Sunday night in August, my first visit to the rehabilitation center, though I had gone regularly to the hospital. He was wearing a sweatshirt instead of his corduroy jacket, a simple navy blue sweatshirt and sweatpants. "They taught me how to dress myself with one hand," he said. I felt a mix of anger and revulsion at seeing this learned and wise man, who had always insisted on being his own master, subject to the rules of a desensitized nursing staff and the constant blare of the television from the bed next to his. I wheeled him into the empty cafeteria where the vending machines were. He wanted a yogurt. I had to open it for him because he could not use his left hand. He commented more as a curiosity than a complaint that when he went home he would not be able to eat a yogurt on his own because he would not be able to open it. We put it down on the table and he ate it with the spoon in his right hand and afterwards I pushed him into the garden.

He found optimism from the things that had remained the same. His face, his mind, his right hand. These are not small things.

It was an August night when the humidity goes and the summer breeze turns cool and the city sky is a dark moonless blue. It was quiet in the garden. We were the only ones there. He had his stock reserve of conversation starters: "What are you reading?" "Heard any jokes?" "How's the writing?" Always "the Writing," as if the *w* should be capitalized. Others will ask, what are you writing? Are you writing? He knew better. He knew it was about process. I began to talk about *Soldier in the Grass*, a little hesitantly at first, because it seemed trivial compared to his ordeal. But he seemed sincerely interested and I wanted to talk about it. This was my first attempt at writing since my daughter was born, and I felt this strange trepidation, strangely out of touch with the emotions that had inspired my writing in the past. I was not sure that I would ever write again. He also had those fears then.

Sitting together in the dark garden at the Terence Cardinal Cooke Health Center I told him the story that was taking shape in my head. This continued over the course of the next few Sunday nights. He would listen and comment, and the story took on life.

One Sunday night when I arrived he had good news. He said he was going home that week. "I had to accept that I would never walk again. I will not have the use of my left arm. Once I accepted that I was fine," he said. "I can go on."

He had all the flaws one finds in the saints, the unwillingness to compromise and the acceptance of suffering that leads as easily to self-destruction as to redemption.

The stroke left him paralyzed on his left side. He returned to his apartment on the second floor of a walkup, wheelchair bound and living alone, no elevator, no doorman. The apartment had been professionally cleaned for his return. The idea was mine. One of his students who had been playing a big role in his everyday life at the time arranged for the cleaning. She had failed to be present, however, when it took place. He arrived to find that all of his cameras had been stolen. It was the first disappointment and shock of what this new life of dependence on other people would mean.

He learned how to get by, how to scratch his way out of his Venetian prison with his fingernails like Casanova, and how to find people to help him. When I said I was searching and I found Bill, I was not alone. Everyone who found Bill was searching, the young actresses, disenchanted accountants and lawyers, and above all poets: they all took turns carrying his chair up and down the flight of stairs and wheeling him wherever he needed to go.

He complained, one girl in particular couldn't wheel the chair without hitting too many bumps and the bumps were painful. Another girl came late to take him to class. As time went on, the more needy he became, the more demanding. He became increasingly frustrated, irritated, the irritation turned quickly to anger.

He filled his days with writing plays and watching movies on an old television. He typed with one hand. He smoked. "If I die from smoking I accept it," he said. "I won't feel sorry for myself." Just as he accepted being paralyzed. He stopped physical therapy. "I will never get better. I have to accept that."

Our friendship could not be the way it had been in the

past. No more frequent meetings in the coffee house on Greenwich Avenue; I couldn't help him down the stairs of his apartment building by myself. No more long telephone conversations late at night. He hadn't enough breath to sustain those conversations. The pauses were no longer a space for thought but a gasp for air.

I visited him once on a frigid Saturday morning in winter. He had called me a few times during the week to ask whether I was coming. Finally he just said it: if I didn't, he was going to be alone until Sunday afternoon. I told him I would be there at noon. He needed to know the precise time because it was hard for him to open the door to his apartment and he needed to make preparations in advance. Though it was a sunny day, in his apartment it was dark, and he had only the desk lamp with the exposed bulb shining directly on the desk next to the television. I brought him a hamburger, fries and a Diet Coke from McDonald's because he liked those things. He ate the fries and sipped the Diet Coke and saved the hamburger for later on. I also brought two videos, *Devil's Advocate* and *Any Given Sunday*. We spoke about *Soldier in the Grass*, though there was no draft at that point worth showing to anyone. I was struggling with something in the story and talking about it with him helped; he knew how to get over the blocks. Mostly he talked and I listened. Then after about an hour he stopped and said gently, "Go home, go back to your daughter."

He had taken to writing short plays, one act, one or two scenes. He would send them to me in the mail. I must have received at least ten in this period. Ordinarily there was no follow-up. No, "Did you like it? What did you think?" There was only one time he called about a play. "Did you read the play I sent you?" I said *no* in a short litany of excuses. He cut me off. "Read the play." He was emphatic. I got off the phone and read it then. A middle-aged man looks at the ceiling as he is making love to a woman half his age. He thinks of all the things the ceiling had witnessed over the years, all the girls who had been in that bed, all the things that had been said, the promises that had been made and broken, the girls who had come and gone. I called him up to tell him how much I liked it. "I knew you would. I know my writing isn't really your thing. It's too gritty for you. I knew you'd like this. That's why I wanted you to read it."

He saw the irony in his infirmity. "My plays are being performed because I am in a wheelchair," he would say, and then he'd laugh, as if the wheelchair were making him famous. He was working very hard, writing to fill in the spaces, to escape the boredom and the confinement that came along with his wheelchair.

There was a heart attack, another hospitalization. When I went to see him this time, he told me that he had made up his mind; he was never going back to a hospital.

A year later, seemingly out of nowhere, he lashed out at me. I had called to find out how he was feeling, and rather than answer the phone, he sent me an angry note on the back of a postcard telling me not to call again. Though I was hurt, I believed I understood why he was so angry with me. His resentment must have been growing for a long time. The phone calls were no use to him. He wanted me to visit him more, and I seemed always to find an excuse not to go.

I threw the postcard out. It seemed the sad end of our long friendship, and I did not want to remember those angry words as his last after twenty years.

A few months later he called me. He had no recollection of being angry with me. He seemed surprised that he had told me to stop calling. "Did I say that? I'm sorry, love."

Something had happened and he sought my legal advice. It seemed a lawsuit might be the only way of redressing his problem. In that first conversation he did not want to sue. A few days later he called back; he had decided to take action, even if it meant a lawsuit. Over the course of the next few months he called once a week; these were always short conversations about what progress was being made in his legal matter. I could hear how sick he was. I heard him struggling for breath.

As summer turned to September and then October without a resolution he became frustrated. His frustration turned to anger. He had no money to pay for his "heart medication," as he referred to it. I told him I would go to his pharmacy on Sunday and pay for the medicine. This calmed him and he was able to talk about other things. He must have asked me if I was writing. I told him I had just finished a draft of the novel we had spoken about a few years before. He offered to read it.

I had completed three earlier novels, each edited by Bill, often in more than one draft. Knowing how sick he was, I would not have asked him this time, but he offered and it meant so much to me.

It was a wintry Sunday afternoon in October. An early chill was in the air and the sky was a low, gray cover. After going to the pharmacy, I met Bill in the coffee shop on Seventh Avenue and 15th Street. He was seated at his usual table in the front. I had not seen him in a while. I did not recognize any of the people at the table with him, though they were seated around him like disciples. As they talked, his eyes were fixed on the television screen. His detachment struck me; it was unlike him. He perked up a little when I sat down, introducing me to everyone at the table, but after a while he went back to watching the football game. In addition to the medicine I brought him a video of a French movie I thought he would like, blank postcards I had brought back from Antibes for him the summer before and the draft of *Soldier in the Grass*.

A few days later I received a note from him typed on the back of one of the postcards.

Great seeing you today, thanks for medication...—will begin going over SOLDIER IN THE GRASS ms...keep me informed. love B Packard

It was dated October 13, 2002.

By the end of the week I had good news. A settlement had been reached in his legal matter. The agreement had to be signed and notarized by him and returned within ten days. We arranged to meet on Monday afternoon to execute the agreement.

There were four of us, three lawyers and one off-duty Park policeman, that Monday afternoon as we wheeled Bill around the neighborhood looking for a notary. The date was October 21st. There was nothing on Seventh Avenue so we went over to Sixth. Bill seemed withdrawn, sitting with the blanket over his legs gazing straight ahead. The sun was shining in his eyes and he had no way of avoiding it. He scarcely said a word. It never occurred to us that finding a notary would prove so difficult. The only notary we found claimed he was too busy. We went to a few more places to no avail. It was getting late, close to five, and we all had to be somewhere. Though I was insisting it had to be done then, we had run out of options in the neighborhood and Bill could not travel by taxi. We were standing on the corner of 14th Street and Sixth Avenue making plans to meet on Thursday when I saw the notary who had refused us an hour before heading into the subway. I stopped him and managed to persuade him to go back to the store and notarize the document. As we were waiting Bill discreetly asked if he could borrow some cash to get him through the week. I gave him what I had, though I could tell he was disappointed. We were all in a rush at that point. There was a hurried good-bye on the corner of 14th Street and Sixth Avenue.

That Friday he called to say that he had finished *Soldier in the Grass*. He insisted that he wanted to get the manuscript with his comments into my hands right away. There was something pressing in his insistence. The following Monday morning he called anxious to know whether I agreed with his changes. I told him he had seen things that no one else would have seen or known how to fix. He responded with detached satisfaction, "I guess that's right. I am the best editor of fiction out there."

He made me assure him that I would put the changes through right away because there was someone he wanted to send it to. Before he hung up he told me that he loved me and that I had been a good friend.

That Sunday Raymond Hammond called to tell me Bill had passed away. His edit of *Soldier in the Grass* was among his final contributions to the life of writing that he loved so much. "It's a good life," he would say. "When the writing is going well and the words are dancing across the page, it's a joy like no other."

I remember what Bill said about the soldier: "In the end he was satisfied."

THE SOLDIER IN THE GRASS

I was astonished at what an overwhelmingly heartfelt powerful
story this is - heroic episodic Saga which records the dreadful
ordeal of realization of two lost & lonely souls who find
each other in the blasting heat of Africa as they journey
towards their ultimate destination.

Your research is awesome and reader can really feel the lazy
and luxurious foliage of Africa - the stasis of stillness in
noontime heat. But beyond the research, god knows how you know
so much about Africa, guns, medicine, voodoo, the French
Foreign Legion, &c.

I feel the presence of 2 authors or their style in your writing -
Henry James for the impeccable detail perceptions, and Hemingway
for shocking action narrative. I'd prefer less James and more
Hemingway in the rewrite but that's your own choice as you
hammer out your own voice.

Basic problem in rewrite is to cut hell out of chapter two -
its disproportionate length & wordiness can be seen by comparing
chapter lengths in beginning of mss:

            chapter one - 2 pages
            chapter two - 7 pages
            chapter three - 2 pages
            chapter four - 4 pages
            chapter five - 5 pages
            chapter six - 3 pages
            chapter seven - 6 pages
            chapter 8 - 3 pages

You are at your best in short 2-3-4 page chapters, and novel
tends to drag in the 6-7-8 chapters.

I'd also break up the longish paragraphs into separate units,
and insert asterisk separations (* * *) between chapter beats.

I'd say one more rewrite should do the job - turn the story into
a blockbuster read for anyone..

Certain locutions get on my nerves - I know you're using the French
version of infermerie but its repetition makes one wish you used
the English infirmary spelling.

Following are notes on separate chapters together with typos,
misspellings, and word choice problems.

10.25.02

2229287BV00006B/3/P
27 August 2009
Breinigsville, PA USA